From Across the Waters

by

Richard Neil LaBute Jr.

DORRANCE PUBLISHING CO
EST. 1920
PITTSBURGH, PENNSYLVANIA 15238

Dorrance Publishing Co
585 Alpha Drive
Pittsburgh, PA 15238
Visit our website at *www.dorrancebookstore.com*

ISBN: 978-1-4809-3156-5
eISBN: 978-1-4809-3133-6

I dedicate this, my second novel, to my dear mother, Marian La Bute-Stone. My mother has had a lifelong love of reading, oftentimes historical genre, and must have instilled in me this love of reading and of books somewhere along the way.

Also, I want to thank my dear friends Mary Ellen Gutknecht, Kay Horntvedt, Sue Wright and especially Dave Wright for their time and effort in reviewing and commenting on the draft. Their collective help is very much appreciated!

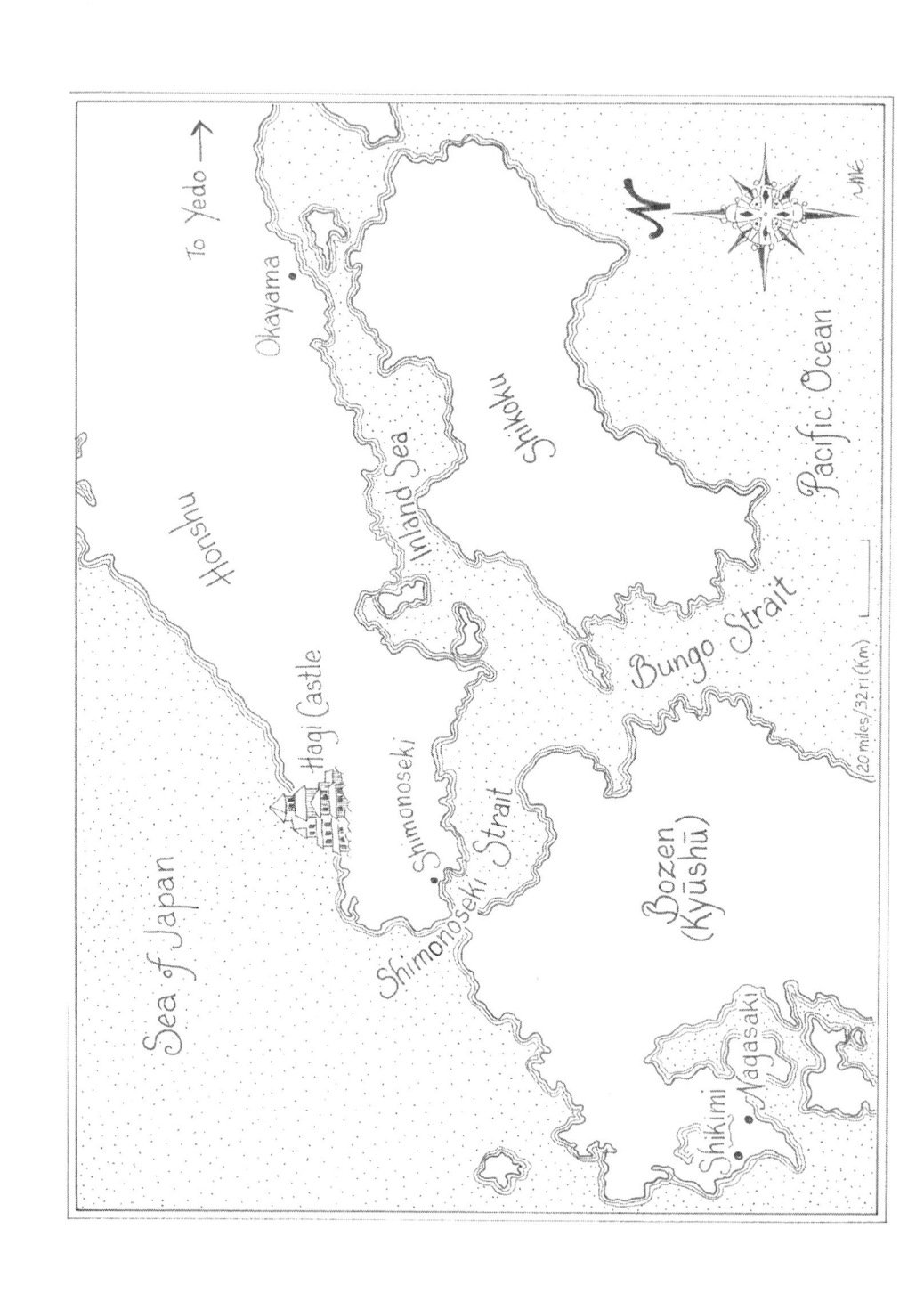

From Across the Waters

Chapter One
Jiro

aster spy Ueno Jiro never really retired or even intended to retire. Along with the gradual loss of his eyesight, and more importantly, his acute sense of hearing, he is unable to keep pace with the rapid and monumental changes overtaking his homeland. Since the Restoration and the ensuing years under the Emperor Meiji, Japan has been transformed from a feudal backwater of semi-autonomous fiefdoms to a modern nation. A nation of steam power, blue-water ships, railroads, telegraph and laws. The last of the samurai have surrendered their arms and armor and have submitted to Imperial authority or have been slaughtered where they stood. Jiro hedged his bets correctly and made a seamless, more importantly, unnoticed transition from an underestimated snitch of the *bakufu*, Tokugawa-era government, to a highly respected master spy of the new regime.

Ueno Jiro is a polyglot in Japanese, English, Dutch and Portuguese. He possesses a razor-sharp mind honed during his many years of Shogunate and Imperial service. Now, he is unable to continually update his skill set and constantly reestablish his credentials with an ever-younger line of bureaucrats and keepers. He still receives a small stipend and is consulted, although less and less frequently, until his irrelevance becomes self-evident.

Relevant or irrelevant, this all depends on a point of view. Many years past, a priest had admonished him in saying, "All the gods matter, just as all men matter." This thought, among other thoughts, snippets and memories, the mental litany of his life, comfort and satisfy him in his eighty-ninth year. He sits on a comfortable *zabuton*, traditional Japanese cushion, sipping hot *sake*, rice wine, at the hearth of the house of his father. Here the memories of his mother, his brothers, his first travels overseas in the warship of the *gaijin*, foreigner, Commodore Perry, a functionary of the *bakufu* and years in the governmental organs of the Meiji Emperor warm him. These fill him with pride and satisfaction. He closes his eyes, smiles and passes from this world to the next.

Gonohe, the fifth gate, was a village then, but an important village on the *Tohoku*, northern district, road in the *Michinoku*, end of the road, district of Japan. Many years before, the ruling *Tokugawa* clan erected a series of *mon*, customs gates, along the north-south road in order to regulate commerce and to collect taxes, a tax collection process which, on occasion, departed from just governance and bordered on extortion. The timeless question being which is worse, highwaymen or government officials, remains poignant to this day. In any event, *Gonohe* was one of these dozen or so customs-gate villages.

In the twenty-sixth year of the reign of Emperor Ninko (1843), perhaps two hundred families comprising a thousand souls inhabited

Gonohe proper. Here the people live as they have always lived, subordinate to their feudal lord, who in turn paid homage and conducted the local government on behalf of his liege lord, Tokugawa Ieyoshi, the *Shogun* himself. But the *Shogun* and his capitol of *Yedo*, modern Tokyo, were sixteen hundred *ri* away; that is over eight hundred kilometers when measured in the traditional way of one *ri* equaling one half kilometer. Sixteen hundred *ri* from the mountain village of *Gonohe* is a considerable distance when walking or pulling a handcart. Here conveyance options are limited in a land where horses are expensive and the exclusive property of great and noble lords and where wagons are forbidden on government roads.

Lord Sumida, the *bushi*, samurai warlord, granted title to this village and its surrounding lands, dispenses justice on behalf of the *bakufu*, ruling bureaucracy in *Yedo* and in accordance with his own whims or particular digestion.

The village is nestled in a mountain valley, and is seen clearly from any one of several surrounding peaks. The bisecting north-south road is visible, as is the great *mon* of *Gonohe*. The proud village boasts a beautiful *jinja*, Shinto shrine complex, a dozen or so two-story, wood-frame family businesses, sundry hundred or so traditional *kaiyabukiyane*, thatched-roof dwellings, and of course, the great manor of Lord Sumida.

It is into this typical, rural *Yedo-jidai*, Tokugawa-era, setting that we find *bakufu* functionary Ueno Takeji and his wife, Masako, conducting their lives and raising their four sons in accordance with all the traditional and cultural expectations of Japan's early nineteenth-century feudal society.

Ueno Jiro is born the second son in the Ueno household. As second son he can expect no inheritance and little more than the family name with which to find his way in the world. As a young boy, of course, he is unaware of his limited avenues, but is quick to discover the things that most young boys discover: the delights of exploration, the disappointments of trial and error, punishment and hardest of all, adult expectations.

Jiro tends not to be as social as the other boys in *Gonohe*. His intellectual capacity separates him from others in ways he does not yet understand. He does enjoy an activity when invited, but prefers his time alone, in the mountain forest, fishing for *aiu*, Japanese sweetfish, in the river or better yet, *iwana*, brook trout, in the mountain streams.

Formal education is generally not available to young men of inferior birth, particularly those from isolated rural regions like *Tohoku*, where the *han*, clan, of the feudal Japanese warlord, of Lord Sumida had not yet established a school for boys. Still, even as a young boy, Jiro dreams of attending the *Yushima Seido*, Tokugawa-era academy for training young government bureaucrats, in *Yedo*. Jiro's answer to low birth is to loiter around the local *jinja*, befriend the priests and feign interest in religious affairs. Subsequently, Jiro is rewarded by earning the goodwill of the resident priests which he leverages into access and a chance to learn calligraphy and reading, even if this means too much rote memory of less than interesting religious dogma and chants. Still, Jiro's young mind is learning! At the age of ten, Jiro is already honing his intellect and practicing the art of deception in order to cater to his own desires.

"Jiro, who were the first three gods to inhabit the High Plain of the Earth?" asks the chief priest of the *Gonohe jinja*.

"The *Nihon Shoki*, the Chronicles of Japan 720 A.D., teach us that three gods were the first to inherit and inhabit the High Plain of the Earth, *sensei*, teacher," replies Jiro.

"Three gods? Who were they? Name them, Jiro."

"*Ame-no-minaka-mushi-no-kami*, the solitary deity is the most important god, *sensei*, teacher or master. Do the others matter?"

"Impertinence will be your undoing, Jiro. All gods matter, just as all men matter! Study harder and do not allow your mere superficial understanding of the scriptures and quick wit govern your answers in the future. I may accept your half-answer this time, but not forever! Beware of your tongue," replies a bemused yet annoyed chief priest Sato-*san*.

"Thank you, *sensei*," replies Jiro, smiling to himself as he bows deeply to the chief priest. "I must return home now. May I come back tomorrow?"

"Yes, Jiro. You are always welcome here in the House of the gods. Good day to you, son."

"Good day, *sensei*. Thank you for your benevolent and guiding hand."

Jiro carefully, but quickly, returns the scripture rolls to their rightful place in the shrine. He reverently bows before the *shaden*, Shinto alter, skips out the door and runs down a packed dirt trail leading from the *jinja* to the road below. As the side street merges with the great north-south road, Jiro observes a throng of people, some laden with cargo making their way in both directions. He wonders from where they come, where they are going and why? What is concealed in those carefully wrapped bundles and boxes? What mysteries are there to be uncovered here in plain sight? At just ten years old, Jiro's mind yearns for the knowledge of what is hidden from view, in this, a society where, **what is not to be seen is unseen, what is not to be heard is unheard and what is not to be known is unknown.**

Jiro returns home this day, walking along the great north-south road thinking these thoughts of every passerby.

Given the close physical proximity of Japanese society, be things unseen, unheard and unknown, still a promising young man does not go unnoticed. And so it is to be with Jiro, that before the beginnings of his manhood, Lord Sumida, always looking for prospective military and bureaucratic talent, offers to accept young Jiro into his greater household for training and observation. Time and observation would then dictate a future for the young man.

"*Tadaima*," coll. just now, "I'm home," yells Jiro as he noisily slides open, then slides shut the door behind him.

"*Okaerinasai*, welcome home, Jiro. Where have you been? Your father is looking for you," replies his mother, Masako.

"Jiro? Is that you, Jiro? Come in here, sit. I wish to speak with you," commands his father, Takeji.

This is most unusual. Jiro senses something, but what? He hasn't any particular transgressions to confess or amends to make, yet his father summons him. Could it be a reprimand for his flippant answer to Sato the priest? Impossible, even the gods do not travel so fast! Still, it is something. Something is coming his way.

"Ah, Jiro, my second, yet most promising son. I have good news for you. Our liege lord, Lord Sumida, has noticed you."

"Noticed me, Father?"

"Yes, my son, noticed you." Replies Takeji again, somewhat more sharply. "Lord Sumida has agreed to accept you into his stable of young men for training in martial arts and administration. He has greatly honored this house with this offer, and affords you a tremendous opportunity for a future. Let us thank the gods!"

"Yes, Father. I will be sure to thank the gods. When am I to leave?"

"Jiro, you are to pack your things at once. Say your goodbyes to your brothers and mother this evening after supper and report to Lord Sumida's stable tomorrow morning."

A silent tear runs down Jiro's cheek; his shoulders perceivably heave. He is not sad to leave his family, only sorry to leave familiar surroundings, surroundings of which he is master. Before he can finish the thought, his father Takeji's course voice interrupts.

"Jiro, stop that whimpering! It is unseemly. Go and prepare yourself. Do your family honor."

Jiro departs his father's presence for "his" room, a room shared by all his brothers. Masako has prepared a fine meal to celebrate the family's good fortune. Rice and *tsukemono*, pickled vegetables, are a daily staple, but tonight the evening meal is augmented by *iwana*, brook trout marinated in sweet sake and soy sauce, fried *tofu*, soy cakes, and a thin broth with mountain vegetables and noodles, all of Jiro's favorite dishes.

Still the boy, be he, man of the hour, is strangely silent with his sudden "good" fortune. He ponders his prospects in Lord Sumida's compound, two *ri* distant, an another world away.

Sleeplessly Jiro lies warmly between his brothers wondering what the morrow will bring. As sleep finally, mercifully dulls his senses, the cock crows, the *jinja* bell rings and life begins to stir in the village. Deprived of sleep, his body heavy with fatigue, Jiro resists rising, but is goaded by his brothers who are already arguing, posturing, dressing and preparing for the day ahead. Jiro has no choice in the matter, he too must rise and face his "big" day. Comforted by the smell and thought of *asagohan*, morning rice, hot *misoshiru*, bean paste broth garnished with white radish or mushrooms, a soft-boiled egg, *tsukemono* and tea, he rises to face the day.

Jiro carefully folds and places his few possessions into a *furoshiki*, cloth wrapper, rearranges the bedding he has already placed away in the closet and takes one last look at "his" room. He will most likely never sleep here again.

Asagohan bolsters his spirits somewhat, but all too soon the time has come to depart. He picks up his small belongings, bows slightly to his siblings, more deeply to his mother Masako and finally to the *kamidana*, family shrine. He does not look his mother in the eye, lest he betray the tears welling up and blurring his sight.

Finally, with concerted self-control, he says, "Goodbye, Mother. Goodbye, all." He then turns and heads down the packed-dirt street leading to the great north-south road. Though his journey today is short, as he joins the main road, the thought occurs to him, "Today I am one of the baggage-laden travelers walking south on the great road." The thought cannot but bring a small smile to his face. The smile remains for a time. Today the morning is quiet, the day is mild and as by nature and practice, he begins observing others on the road. This pleasant fiction soon dissipates, however, as he approaches the two-meter-high wall of wood and stone which surrounds the great manor of Lord Sumida.

"Kode!" The *Kendo*, Japanese sword martial art, wrist attack movement.

The swish, snap and pain which barely proceed the word, as the *Kendo shinai*, bamboo practice sword, falls sharply on Jiro's wrist. Only three days into his new surroundings at Lord Sumida's stable and he is exhausted. Exhausted from the physical training, unfriendly hazing, and awkward integration into the house of the feudal lord. Food is plentiful, but not tastily prepared like that of Jiro's mother. Friendships are even harder to come by in a stable of competitive boys ever trying to outdo the other and catch the eye of a trusted servant, instructor or even Lord Sumida himself.

Jiro studies hard; he has to. Jiro has to make up for his lack of formal education. It was so much easier to verbally joust and mentally outwit the priests at the shrine. Jiro carefully watches each count of each movement in *Kendo* practice. He has already mentally devised a new defense based on the principals and movements of the art—now for a chance to put his defense into practice.

Jiro does not have long to wait. Within a fortnight, Goh, the inbred and overfed assistant martial arts instructor, has decided to take out his hangover on the new stable of boys at practice.

"Today I will demonstrate a coordinated movement using two *shinai*, one long and other short, simulating a *katana*, Japanese long sword and a *tanto*, Japanese short sword, attack.

"Kiyoshi, you are first."

Nervously Kiyoshi steps out from the closely packed group of boys. He positions himself, right foot forward, several paces back and centered on Goh. Kiyoshi raises his *shinai*, handgrip near his navel, end of the stick pointing up at a forty-five degree angle, poised for attack or defense.

"Araah!" Goh leaps forwards swinging the *shinai* in his right hand in a great arcing motion, followed by the shorter stick in his left in a thrusting motion. Crack, crack. Both sticks hit their marks. Kiyoshi accidentally drops his *shinai* as his skull and side throb with pain.

"*Bakamon*, idiot! Kiyoshi, you are an idiot. Pick up your *shinai*. You are a disgrace, a stench in my nostrils."

"Jiro! You are next." Jiro emerges from the gaggle of boys. Jiro also positions himself as Kiyoshi did. More fodder for Goh.

"Araah!" Goh attacks again. Jiro deftly arcs his body backward while standing his ground. Goh's swing and thrust miss their mark, yet momentum carries him forward. Jiro recovers his original position and thrusts up directly into Goh's throat. "*Tsuki,*" throat thrust, screams Jiro. A perfect throat thrust. Goh drops to his knees writhing in pain. He too drops his *shinai*, as did Kiyoshi. Jiro can predict Goh's embarrassed anger. He can expect *shikai-ishi*, vengeance, from Goh. Jiro feigns clumsiness as he steps back, bows and meekly asks, "*sensei*, how can one properly defend oneself from such a fearsome attack?" Goh, still clutching his throat, tears of pain welling from his slightly bulging eyes, croaks, "*Tsuki.*" Jiro bows his head as if in supplication, smiles to himself and returns to his new and exalted place among the stable boys.

Chapter Two
David

Retired Rear Admiral David McDougal never married again. Since his wife's needless death in 1863, David has been unable to consummate the physical act of love, impotent in both body and soul, and now, with age, indifferent to the effort.

Full-bearded, he sits in a chair, legs covered with a blanket, smoking a cigar, staring out across the waters of the Chesapeake from his porch near Leonardstown, Maryland. He sees that which is visible, some that is invisible, all through the cloudy blue haze of his old eyes. What is not clearly in focus, he draws from memory, for the Chesapeake has not changed, only he has changed. David has been worn away by sea salt, weather, and men. Each of the elements of his exposure has claim to a piece, a line or a white hair on his person.

Never a slight man, since his retirement in 1871, "The Admiral" has out-grown both uniform and Sunday best. A loose fitting shirt and overalls now suit him best. Swollen ankles and shortness of breath indicate that he is worn-out on the inside as well. Death should come painlessly one night. Suddenly, the comforting thought is punctuated by throbbing and a sharp pain in his head. He loses control or consciousness and finds himself prostrate on the floor of the porch unable to move or even cry out.

David whimpers in pain. Drool mixed with tobacco juice and blood seep from his mouth. He has injured himself in the fall. He soils himself. Death does not appear on cue; night falls. He is cold. Morning does not come, only fleeting memories of soldiers, sailors and marines he has seen, contorted, crumpled, prostrate as he, on the battlefield and on deck.

Ultimately we are all dead men. He dies just before dawn, not lost at sea or in a tomb of unknown, but on the fertile ground which is his beloved Maryland.

"David, stop daydreaming and finish your lesson! Or, have you already completed the assignment? Perhaps you would like to read to the class your letter to the President in regards to Captain Lewis' overland expedition to the Pacific Ocean."

David breaks from his gazing at Chesapeake Bay, and rediscovers himself, stylus in hand, sitting at his schoolhouse desk with Miss Madson and the class staring back at him expectantly.

"Yes, Miss Madson, my letter to the President is complete. May I read it?"

Dear Mr. President,

I am a student in the class of Miss Madson near Leonardstown in Maryland. We have been assigned the subject of the great overland expedition of Captain Lewis during the presidency of Thomas Jefferson. Further, we are to write a letter to you, Mr. President, and ask what lessons of national significance were learned from the expedition.

Historically we know that the expedition was a survey of the land purchased from the Republic of France in 1803. We also know that Captain Meriwether Lewis and Lieutenant William Clack's Corps of Discovery surveyed the land and waterways along the route, and carefully documented the indigenous peoples, plants and animals. But what we, Miss Madson's class, do not know, is what lessons were learned from the expedition? Where are the physical samples gathered during the expedition? Are these available for public examination? Are more official expeditions planned during your, the Monroe, adminis-tration? These are some of the questions raised in Miss Madson's class. We thank you for any answers you may be able to provide us.

Respectfully submitted,
David S. McDougal

"Very good, David. I must confess, I am rather surprised by your mastery of the subject matter and your fine example of a letter to the President. I misjudged your attention. Has anyone else completed the lesson? Mary Lou, we should be pleased to hear your letter."

As Miss Madson and the class turn their attention to Mary Lou, and before she is halfway through her short letter, David is lost once again in thought, drifting back "out there," somewhere in the Chesapeake Bay.

At three o'clock, the school bell rings, class is dismissed, and the children scramble for home. David is no exception. When he arrives home, he will do his chores like any other boy, or man for that matter. He doesn't mind chores. His chores are no different than those of any family engaged in subsistence farming: feed the animals, milk the cow, cut or bring in some wood for cooking and warmth, or both. He does his chores in a routine, somewhat detached manner. It is not out of boredom or lack of interest necessarily, just that he, at ten years old, is already "out there" seeking something else. After chores, and as daylight permits, David hurries down to the water's edge. Exploring, of course, is the ever-constant motivation, but release from the never-diminished list of chores requires a more pragmatic excuse.

"Ma, I've finished up with chores. Going down to the bay to check the crab pots. Might take a pole along and see if'n I can snag a striper or a blue."

"All right Davie, but be back before dark. Your father doesn't like to wait on his supper."

Suppers on the McDougal farmstead are usually better than most. Ma is an exceptional cook with skills far beyond standard farm fare. Depending on the season and the generosity of the Bay, McDougal suppers are near banquet affairs. Tonight, Chesapeake Bay oyster stew and freshly baked rye bread are in the offer, a meal not to be missed.

Changing from his school clothes, second best after his Sunday best, David wears worn, patched, and comfortable farm clothes, the clothes he likes best.

The pathway to the eastern shore of the bay is worn, worn first by beast, then by indigenous man and finally by the fifth-grade son of a Scot-Irish immigrant. No matter, the light earth and stones of the pathway are indifferent to whose feet tread upon them on their way to the water's edge.

The shoreline along the eastern edge of the great Chesapeake Bay is shallow and thick with reeds and undergrowth. In the Bay's deeper waters schools of migratory bluefish and seabass swim just above acre upon acre of delicious oysters clinging to its bottom. Partially shaded and hidden amongst the brushy outcroppings, debris and weeds are an abundance of smaller fish, shrimp, crabs and clams. "Officially," David's foraging along the shore is for the highly-prized Maryland blue crab. This plentiful, medium-sized crustacean whose sweet tender meat-strands often prove difficult to separate from its shell, but it is the main ingredient in what will become Maryland's signature culinary dish, Maryland crab cakes.

While checking and gathering from his crab traps, David surreptitiously scans the shore, the bay and the horizon, looking amongst the familiar for the new or unfamiliar. David has gathered a half-dozen blue crabs, he'll need many more, when he stops to watch a large sloop sail up the bay. David wonders who pilots the vessel. From whence does he come? What cargo or treasure does she carry concealed in her hold? He stands watching the vessel, then its sail, until only the smallest tip of it is visible above the waves. The sloop disappears over the horizon as darkness begins to descend.

Oblivious to the time, only prompted by darkness, David slings the gunny sack, half-filled with crabs, onto his back and heads for home. Hopefully, his scolding will be mitigated and stayed in recognition of a fine catch.

"Davie, is that you? My stars, Davie, if you ask me, it sure took you long enough to check a few crab traps! Your father wouldn't wait, so you'll have to eat here in the kitchen. You did bring some crabs now, didn't you?"

"Yes, of course, ma it's me! And yes, I did. I brought you a half a sack full of nice blues. Didn't catch any fish though. Guess they're not running yet."

"David, after supper your father would like a word with you."

"Aw, ma. How mad is he? I wasn't that late."

"No, you weren't that late, not for you. But I guess he has something else he wishes to discuss with you."

David quickly devours the proffered oyster stew and bread. The taste of butter lingers in his mouth, not only from the stew, but from the generous portion spread on the warm, hearth-baked bread. Slowly, with trepidation-infused, deliberate steps, he moves toward the sitting room. There the pipe-smoking patriarch of the family waits.

"David, next year you will be graduated from school. Have you given any thought as to your future? Are you interested in remaining here on the farm or apprenticing yourself to a tradesman in Leonardstown? Miss Madson informs me that you have some aptitude in writing. Perhaps I could persuade Mr. MacDonald to take you on at the newspaper as an apprentice."

"Yes, Father. A newspaperman does have some appeal to me."

David retreats quickly from this exchange with his father. He ascends the squeaky Pine board steps to his room in the loft. He changes and goes to bed. Laying there on his pallet, awaiting blissful sleep, the day repeats itself in snapshot-like visions beginning with Miss Matson's classroom. As the events of the day dwindle in his mind, Saturday plans form before these transcend into dreams.

Saturday comes early, illuminating the eastern sky. David rises to meet the day. Leaping down the steps two or three at a time, he grabs a slice of bread left over from the night before and charges into his morning chores.

Sunday, tomorrow, a lifetime away will be consumed by obligatory church service, and the pastor's exhortations of improbable heaven and hell. Church, followed by local social commitments and Sunday "family" time, a euphemism a boring time void of any meaningful activity of interest to a boy. Father will call the family together as he sits smoking his pipe and sipping a drink on the porch or in the sitting room depending on the weather. This is the time Ma will remind and petition him on the many small matters of the week past or the week ahead.

Out the door, down the path again to the water's edge. Without the threat of impending darkness, David baits his hook and throws out his line into the brackish mystery of the bay. David settles into his day. Watching the horizon, the rising and falling of the water on the bay acts as a soothing analgesic to David's soul. His keen sense of observation begins to wane, half-awake, daydreaming, his trace-like state breaks when he suddenly realizes that his bobber is gone. The cane pole line is slack, but the bobber has disappeared among the reeds. David jumps up to investigate.

Walking along the shoreline, scan alternating between shore and shallows, he peers through a thatch of reeds discovering not only his missing bobber, but a half-submerged, debris-filled ketch with two broken masts. It's not much of a ketch, as ketches go, exceedingly small in fact, but what a find!

David is by nature a bit introverted, intense but intense without overt emotion. The discovery of the ketch, however, overwhelms him. He doesn't know whether to shout or cry and longs to share his great luck with someone. He is determined to salvage the boat and decides on the spot to christen it "Ketch of the Day."

Druia McDougal

Chapter Three
Mori

The moment is at hand. Mori Takachika concentrates as he pulls the razor-sharp *tanto*, short sword, from its sheath. Surrounded by the idyllic, peaceful grounds of the family shrine, and witnessed by all the *daijin*, headmen, of the realm, he thrusts the knife to the hilt into his gut and pulls right. Before his lips can utter a sound, Mori's second decapitates him in one quick motion.

Mori's over-sized head falls from his shoulders on the sandy ground with a thud. He is dead. Or is he? For a second or two, the severed head, released from the confines of the body lives on. It perceives light and sound. His lips quiver but do not seem capable of speech. Then, slowly, the light and sound recede. He no longer feels his lips, tongue or eyelids. Nothing. Yes, now he is truly dead, at least to this world, but his *kami*, spirit, is now free to transcend to the next.

The Thirteenth *Daimyo*, Lord, of the *Choshu*, The Prince of *Nagato*, faithful servant of the Son of Heaven and defier of the barbarians, is gone. He has passed from this life to the realm of the dead, one in communion with his ancestors. Ancestors who will be pleased with his demonstrated strength in life, and his atonement and honor in this final act of *seppuku*, ritual suicide.

A message. A message bearing the *mitsuba-aoi mon*, the hollyhock crest of the Tokugawa Shogun, arrives by courier at *Hagi* Castle in western Japan. *Hagi* Castle is the powerful fortress home of the Mori *han*, clan.

> To all who shall see these presents greeting. Know ye that reposing special trust and confidence in our peer Mori Narito, twelfth *daimyo* of the Mori *han* and protector of the *Choshu* Domain, the court hereby extends its favor and protection to his heir, Mori Takachika in hospitality at this court in *Yedo*. Given his application and diligence, the heir, Mori Takachika, can expect to be proffered rank and position in the administration of his Excellency Shogun Tokugawa Ieyoshi.
>
> It is desired that the heir, Mori Takachika, and no more than two retainers arrive in *Yedo* by not later than ninety days upon receipt of this summons.

The twelfth *daimyo* of the Mori *han* sits in the great hall of *Hagi* Castle with Counselor Takahashi carefully contemplating his future as it is extended through the life of his son and heir. The future of the family, the *han* and the *Choshu* Domain may strengthened or weakened with his choice of action.

"To accept the 'summons' of the Shogun and send young Takachika to be 'educated' at the *Yushima Seido* in *Yedo* is tantamount to the capitulation of the *han*," flatly states Lord Mori, staring straight ahead.

"Not to accept the 'offer' of the Shogun will isolate and gradually alienate the *han* from the *bakufu*, government bureaucracy, center of power and your peers. Empowered domains will encroach our borders, unfavorable declarations will be made and eventually will war come to the *Choshu* Domain, *tono-sama*, my lord," counters Counselor Takahashi.

"This is a summons, not an offer, Takahashi. The offer, as you say, is an invitation to incarceration and hostage holding. These are the Tokugawa's favorite methods. I have a choice, but then again I have no choice. You counsel appeasement and patience. I react with indignation and obstinacy. How shall we shall we thread this needle, Takahashi?"

Lord Mori has already decided to counter the offer, with a plot of his own making. After a moment of reflection, Mori continues.

"Takahashi, we will accept and celebrate the invitation on young Takachika's behalf. Order a courier sent immediately to *Yedo* with our enthusiastic acceptance. Then, call for Jedo, my chief assassin."

Carrying a painstakingly calligraphied, sealed letter bearing the *mon* of Lord Mori, as well as a suitably expensive gift, a courier is dispatched in a public and ceremonial manner. Even as the gates of *Hagi* Castle close behind the dispatched courier, Lord Mori secretly meets with Jedo the assassin. Counselor Takahashi sits quietly behind Lord Mori.

"Jedo, in two weeks' time young Takachika and two of his retainers will travel to *Yedo* on the *Tokaido* Road. Take several of your best men. Depart the *Choshu* domain by stealth, then allow others to observe you and your men loitering near the western border of the *Oda* Domain. Assault Takachika's entourage in a very sloppy and brigand-like fashion, kill any witnesses and chase Takachika back toward home. Do you understand?"

"Yes, my lord, I understand. No questions. Your will shall be my mantra, *tono*," pledges Jedo. Jedo bows deeply, repeatedly, and silently departs.

"Upon learning of the incident, I'll send my regrets to the court, noting the attempt on the life of the heir of the *Choshu* Domain, and refuse to send him to *Yedo*. Some may see the improbability of an assassination attempt, others will argue that the *Tokaido* Road is not a safe travel. No firm consensus will be arrived at. The scenario should minimally sow confusion within the *bakufu* and cause delay. We will welcome the delay, eh Takahashi?"

"Very clever, my lord. But will it work?" interjects Counselor Takahashi.

Still sitting in the great hall, Lord Mori summons young Takachika.

"Takachika, as my son and heir to a powerful *han* and the *Choshu* Domain, the Shogun's court in *Yedo* has ordered you to attend the *Yushima Seido* for martial and administrative training. You will, of course, embrace this opportunity and go. Take two retainers and that which you may require for an extended stay. Depart soon, by which I mean, within the week. Travel the *Tokaido* Road only by day. Mingle with common travelers for safety. You may overnight at common inns or seek the indulgence of our neighbors along the way. We are at peace and have reasonable relations with the *Oda* and *Takeda han*. I would not expect trouble. Do you have any questions?"

"No, my Lord Father," says Takachika stoically as he bows and departs. Questions are not for Lord Mori. Questions and answers are to be sought out privately from Counselor Takahashi or other *daijin* of the realm, not the Lord Father. Takachika seeks out Counselor Takahashi.

"Thrust, parry, counter-thrust. So it is in combat, so it is in politics. The master thrives, the fodder dies. The world remains balanced on the back of the turtle," patiently explains Counselor Takahashi to Takachika.

"Yes, I understand the different movements in sword practice, and how this can be likened to politics, but why can't I just stay here like the others," pleads Takachika.

"Because, whether you accept it or not, you are not like the others. You are the only son and heir to an important *daimyo*. Until which time **you** become the *daimyo*, others may try to use you to either influence or hurt your father, Lord Mori. This is your fate. The gods will not allow you escape your fate, here in this life or even in death. Be patient. In time you will see the wisdom of your Lord Father. In time, you will grow more and more in his image. Now, go and pack," counsels Takahashi.

In less than the time allotted by his Lord Father, Takachika assembles those items required for the journey and his expected, lengthy sojourn in *Yedo*. Guided by Counselor Takahashi, preparations are made, and the luggage is loaded onto a pack animals. Although no weapons are allowed at the *Yushima Seido*, Takachika stashes a *tanto* in his clothes as well as his favorite game of *go*, Chinese board game of strategy.

Takachika is unused to being the center of attention, but today the center of attention he is. Himself dressed for a journey, a tutor of Takahashi's choosing, a manservant and two pack animals, the small entourage prepares to depart the courtyard of *Hagi* Castle. The servants, castle guard and family see them off. His mother is unhappy but stoic, his father typically aloof and seemingly uninterested in the event. Takachika senses that this great moment in his young life is almost a non-event to his Lord Father. He cannot help but to wonder, why?

The *Tokaido* Road officially stretches from *Osaka* to *Yedo* via *Kyoto*, the cloistered residence of the Son of Heaven, Japan's Emperor. Fifty-seven government-sanctioned inns, which generally include a porter house and stables as well as rooms, food and bathing, are found along the route. The dreaded *mon*, Tokugawa customs gates, where travel permits and travelers are scrutinized and protection is provided, more often than not, protection of the mafiosa type rather than that of proper law enforcement.

Takachika is old enough to distinguish the mon of the different *han* along his route of travel. With trepidation, he "leads" his little entourage down the road toward *Yedo*.

Chapter Four
Robert

Life, often times, swings full circle. And so it is in the case of Robert H. Pruyn, lawyer, judge, politician, general officer and esteemed statesman. Having returned to the place of his birth and center of his prominent family's influence, Albany in New York, some years before, Robert takes up a popular post-war profession, banking, and eventually, as he rebuilds his wealth, philanthropy. Still only in his fifties, in the course of two decades, he has accomplished much more, travelled farther and borne more various and diverse professional titles than most men would in three lifetimes.

Having lost his dear wife years before the great conflict, the tragedy proved to be the right catalyst, along with the encouragement of his close friend and Lincoln Cabinet member William H. Seward, to depart the shores of America and become the United States emissary to the Court of the Shogun in Japan. Although his years as Representative Minister in

Japan will be his most noteworthy achievement, now he turns his attentions to business pursuits and his son. He is particularly proud of his son, Robert C., who demonstrates aptitude and follows his father into banking. This sharing of the family business burdens, allows Robert to spend time cultivating his first and foremost interest, the law. With others, he founds the Albany School of Law.

Respect, prominence in the community and wealth provide Robert with comfortable distraction. He has been nurturing and generous to others, but in spite of so many successes in life, he still feels loss, emptiness and uncertainty each and every day.

On day in 1882, as by habit and routine, Robert rises early, refreshes, dresses and is served a hearty breakfast. Finishing his meal, he pushes himself away from the kitchen table, crosses the kitchen for the back door. Robert stumbles, and falls. Robert H. Pruyn is dead.

The old New York Village of Beverwijck's name had been changed now for almost a century and a half, but the original Dutch heritage still runs deep in 1825. Though Albany is located one hundred forty-odd miles west of the big city, for the past twenty-eight years now it has been the capital of New York State. This busy transportation hub is nestled at the confluence of the navigable Hudson and Mohawk rivers. It has become known as the political center of the state, but its *raison d'etre*, reason for being, is the steady movement of goods, services and settlers along its rivers and roads. In the year 1825 Albany is the tenth largest city in the fledgling United States of America.

The Pruyn family is well known in Albany, and has been since its founding two hundred years before. Robert Pruyn, a boy of breeding and intelligence, is expected to defend the family name and honor, as well as promulgate the family.

"Why, Father, must I spend my time studying ancient Greek and Latin, whereas the civilized world uses French in diplomatic circles, German in music and mathematics, and English in commerce? Would not my waking hours be more profitably spent pursuing mastery of one or more of these languages?" pleads young Robert.

"We study the classics because they are the foundation of Western civilization. Look to your scriptures! Just as Christ teaches us in the parable of the two builders, Matthew 7:24-27, not to build our house on the sand in a spiritual sense, so we build our intellectual foundation on the language and culture of our common, Western forefathers. Without a foundation in the classics, our intellectual house collapses into a Babel of tribal traditions and dialects. This is why we must endeavor to master the rich history of theatre, rhetoric, science and math, and do so in the languages from which these sprung. Does this make sense to you, Robert?" questions Robert's father.

"Yes, Father. I understand your point. But it is also written that man has but three score and ten years in this life, and I will never be able to complete my foundation studies, let alone my educational house in such a short time!" rebuts Robert.

"Robert, you are impertinent! You may go to your room," scolds his father.

At Albany Academy, Robert is popular with other students in spite of his greater than average intellect.

"Robert, have you completed your essay on the merits of the Erie Canal?" asks Headmaster Hamilton.

"Yes, sir. Shall I present it to the class?"

"By all means, Robert. Please proceed."

"Construction of Erie Canal, hereafter referred to as 'our canal,' began here in Albany in 1817. Officially opened only last month, 'our canal' runs 363 miles from New York City, to Albany, to Buffalo and on to Lake Erie. Owned by the State of New York, "our canal" should allow for the trans-state shipment of bulk goods at up to a ninety-five percent cost savings, not to mention more affordable fares for both local and transiting passengers. It is expected that 'our canal' will greatly benefit New York State and position the Port of New York City to become that largest port and most efficient route inland and to the western territories.

"Chief Engineer Benjamin Wright designed and supervised this modern marvel on the scale of the great pyramids of Egypt and should be honored as such. This student proposes that October 26 be proclaimed Benjamin Wright Day in the City of Albany!"

"Very good, Robert. You have a good working knowledge of the current subject matter, and you make a reasonable and persuasive proposal. I applaud your effort. Who will be next?"

After class is dismissed, Headmaster Hamilton, sitting at his desk, retrieves a clean sheet of paper with the Albany Academy crest and begins to write.

Dear Mr. Pruyn,

As Headmaster of Albany Academy, I believe that it is my responsibility to educate and provide guidance, but also to identify individual potential and to promote the growth of the students placed in my care. It has become apparent to me that Robert possesses great intellectual capacity, quite beyond his years and requires a more challenging learning environment than we are able to provide here at Albany Academy. Accordingly, I have taken the liberty to contact my colleague at Rutgers College, formerly Queens College, in New Jersey to see if some opportunity may be available to him there.

I pray that you will not think me presumptuous in making these queries on Robert's behalf. I look forward to our future discussions on the matter once more information is made available to me.

Your humble servant,
Aloysius Hamilton

Headmaster Hamilton posts the letter the next day, and the countdown begins to Robert's new life outside the confines of hearth and Albany.

Chapter Five
Chizuru

*I*n 1926 the new Emperor, Hirohito, has just ascended the Chrysanthemum Throne. Japan, as a "Victor" Nation, is basking in the post-World War I feel good years. Japan foreign relations are at a relative high point, its economy and people prosper.

Sister Agnes of the Sisters of Charity of the God of the Cross, celebrates her sixty-first year within the peaceful sub-culture which is the convent and her eighty-sixth year of life. In her lifetime, she has witnessed and lived through monumental changes in Japan. Since her birth in a small village near *Nagasaki*, Japan has evolved from a feudal state, survived revolution, seen its Emperor restored to power as titular head of state, established a modern parliamentary system of government, and become a respected member in the family of industrialized nations. But most importantly, Sister Agnes has lived to see the Christian faith return to Japan after almost three hundred years of being forbidden, persecuted and driven from its shores. Her heart leaps with joy as young novices freely enter the convent and professed sisters busy themselves with their work, in the surrounding villages and *Nagasaki* as well. Many of Sister Agnes' original members, consisting entirely of her handmaidens from *Hagi* Castle, have already passed away. The simple white crosses in the courtyard bear silent witness to their years of work and prayer. Sister Agnes herself has relinquished title and responsibilities as Mother Superior. She eats little, speaks less and spends hours in quiet contemplation and prayer.

On a quiet winter's morning, she kneels before the altar, in the unheated, stone-floored chapel. Sister Agnes praises God for the blessings and wonders she has lived to see. She draws from deep within to expose her transgressions to Him. She struggles to clearly identify sinfulness in her words and deeds since her last confession in prayer. Her mind wanders. She is so tired.

Later that day she is discovered, eyes closed, body stiff, kneeling in supplication. Without sin, and by His grace, she has passed from this world to be with Him. She has truly gone in peace to love and serve the Lord.

The small fishing village of *Shikimi* just northwest of *Nagasaki* is an unremarkable place to the passerby. It is home to a small fleet of fishing boats, nestled along the *Shikimi* River flowing down from Mt. *Maidake*. One packed-dirt trail winds along the shoreline of the *Sumo-nada* Sea, and through the village northwest toward *Sasebo* or southeast toward *Nagasaki*.

In the twenty-third year of the reign of Emperor Ninko, 1840, a daughter is born to a family of good blood in this village of *Shikimi*. As is tradition, on the twentieth day after her birth, she is bundled in finest silk, and presented to the priest at *Kaminari jinja*, Shinto shrine, where she is named Chizuru, A Thousand Cranes. Her father, Takazawa Yoshio, a samurai by heritage, carries no weapon, rather an official mandate as customs official and headman of this small place. Yoshio, although a man of his times, has been somewhat influenced by a covert network of Christians and Christian sympathizers, greatly scattered and diminished, but a living legacy to the historical significance the religion played in this area in the early 17th century. The original source of this influence is the designated trader's island of *Dejima*, then the center of Dutch and Portuguese commerce and culture just a few *ri* to the southeast of *Shikimi*. These traders, along with their trade goods and technology, brought with them evangelizing Franciscan brothers and dogmatic Jesuit priests in the case of the Portuguese as well as a more pragmatic and free-spirited Reformist view of Christianity, as would be expected, in the case of the Dutch.

Chizuru is a happy girl in the stable house of a good family. She mingles freely with the other children of the village and learns as they learn about things that matter most to children. In Japan, children are dedicated at a *jinja*, four times; at twenty days, at three, five and seven years. The twentieth year is a dedication to adulthood. Until her second dedication at age three her life is one without restraint. At age three however, she, unlike the children of the village, begins her domestic education in dress, manners, ceremony and calligraphy. She is expected to develop into a lady of quality, quality that will be "auctioned" off to the highest bidder at the opportune moment.

Although never formally introduced, Yoshio is aware that a foreigner often walks along the shoreline trail from *Nagasaki*.

Being a part, however small, of the Tokugawan *bakufu* it is his job to be aware, observe and report matters which could affect the control and balance of the regime. This pale, young *gaijin*, foreigner, with blondish-red hair is a doctor who ministers to the other foreigners living near *Dejima* in *Nagasaki*. He is frequently seen fishing along the shore. This is possible because in recent years, the regime has not strictly enforced its segregation policy of the foreigners. In recent years, some foreigners actually frequent bars, eateries, and particularly the lower-class *shofu*, whores, on the periphery of their island base. Yoshio keeps an eye on him; he doesn't want *gaijin* in *Shikimi*.

By age ten, Chizuru is a vibrant, pretty young girl. Intelligence shines in her big, black eyes. She dresses in fine clothes as her station in life dictates. She is quick to learn the honorific nuances of the Japanese language. She doesn't respond to her father with *unda*, yeh, or *hai*, yes or even *hai, wakarimashita*, yes, I understand, like the other children would. Her reply, with a bowed head and averted eyes, is, *hai, kashikomarimashita otosama:* yes, I completely understand, honorable father. She studies tea, and other ceremonies and is blessed with a steady hand resulting in masterful strokes and characters in calligraphy. Secretly, she learns to read and write. *Hokku*, known now as *haiku* Japanese prose, poetry is a favorite.

> *The spring of my existence is upon me*
> *My soul drinks from the well of knowledge*
> *The gods are pleased with their creation*

Not only are the gods pleased, but indeed are Yoshio and his wife, Eko. Only a year or two more, with her flowering, puberty,

Yoshio may then offer Chizuru to prospective noble persons as a wife or even a consort. The right arrangement could prove advantageous to the house of Takazawa.

When not under scrutiny, Chizuru quickly returns to the teasing, taunting, ever restless girl that she is. One day, her tutor Etsuko, notices a listlessness about her.

"Chiruzu-chan, did you not sleep well last night? You look tired," asks Etsuko

"Yes, *sensei*, I slept well, but I'm so tired today. May we continue our lessons tomorrow?"

"Certainly, Chiruzu-chan. Go, rest."

But rest and another night's slept brings no improvement. A bright red rash covers parts of her body. She coughs. When tea or *tamagosake*, common egg and hot sake remedy, are offered, she has difficulty swallowing. She is feverish.

Chizuru's illness greatly concerns Yoshio and Eko. Eko frets over her child. Yoshio expresses concern about her health but worries more about the loss to the family fortunes should she die. Without discussion or consultation, he calls his most trusted family servant, Saburo.

"Saburo, without a word to anyone, go quickly to *Nagasaki*. On *Dejima* Island inquire after the young *gaijin* doctor. Make him understand that he is urgently needed and will be handsomely rewarded for his effort. Disguise him with hat and cloak. Enter the village at night. Do not allow yourselves to be seen. Now go!" orders Yoshio.

Saburo immediately departs on his orders. The twenty *ri* journey to *Dejima* should take no more than two hours. If he walks briskly, perhaps only an hour and another half.

By midday Saburo disembarks a hired boat on *Dejima* Island. A small island crowded with "temporary" shacks, temporary for the past two hundred years! It does not require much time or query to locate the young Dutch doctor, Dr. Andre van der Heide. Unfathomably, the doctor can speak some Japanese. Low class words certainly, not worthy of a cheap *shofu*, he understands and can be understood! Saburo did not think this possible with the filthy, hairy creatures.

In simple language and gesture, Saburo explains, *Illness, please come*. Dr. Andre hesitates. Saburo insists. "*Tomokaku koi*," no questions just come.

Just after dark, they arrive in *Shikimi*. Staying off the main thoroughfare, they make their way to the Takazawa manor. At the *genkan*, threshold, the *gaijin* removes his disguise as well as his shoes. Saburo stands and stares. How is it possible that this *gaijin*, this barbarian, could actually behave like a civilized person? Dr. Andre is led to Chizuru's floor pallet.

Chizuru's swollen throat allows no words to pass, but her eyes see, what the others in the room cannot or are unwilling to see – kind selflessness in the pale blue eyes of the *gaijin* doctor. A quick inspection of the patient confirms a fear – measles. Highly contagious, sometimes deadly, he hurries the lookers-on out of the room.

Dr. Andre applies cool, wet linens to Chizuru to help reduce rash and fever. He coaxes her repeatedly to drink lukewarm tea. After a time, as she sleeps, he removes a simple gold cross from around his neck and places it instead around hers. He prays:

Onze vader die in die hemel zijt

Uw naam worde geheiligd
Our father who art in heaven
Hallowed be thy name

Chapter Six
Yushima Seido

*A*lmost as if in a dream, Jiro stands inside the gates in front of the *Yushima Seido* in *Yedo*. How many years has it been since he lived in his father's house in *Gonohe*, sleeping in one room with his four brothers? How many times did Goh, the martial arts instructor at Lord Sumida's manor, bruise him with a *shinai* in the *dojo*, martial arts practice ring? How his legs ached for most of the sixteen hundred *ri* which he walked up the *Tohoku* Road from *Gonohe* to *Yedo*. But now, he, Ueno Jiro, will finally begin his official education, education at the famous *Shohei-zaka Gaku-monjo*, Neo-Confucian High School operated by the Tokugawan Shogunate, at *Yushima Seido*!

Jiro walks slowly toward the colonnaded entrance to the giant Cedar-shaded building, the so-called Hall of Sages. A man is standing there to greet, him? The rector, the *Daigaku no kami*, head of the chief educational institution of the state, Hayashi Sokan stands in front of the door under the portico skeptically

45

evaluating this hayseed from *Gonohe*. Making a mental note, Hayashi's lips move as he talks to himself. "Much has been said about this upstart, we shall see."

Having but few possessions, Jiro requires little in terms of space or comfort. Still, the student's living quarters can hardly be called comfortable, dining hall only adequate and classrooms, institutional.

Not specializing in any particular subject matter, Jiro's powers of observation and strong memory serve him well here at the *Shohei-zaka Gakumonjo*. He is quick on the uptake, and within a short period of time becomes well known as a bright generalist. He excels at Geography, Contemporary Affairs, and *Kokugo*, Japanese language. Foreign languages are not curricular subjects in a Japan still officially operating under the *sakoku*, Tokugawan isolation policy. Japan sits in geographic and self-imposed isolation, yet Jiro's mind yearns to break these bureaucratic imposed boundaries, although he doesn't even realize this yet.

In mid-August is *obon*, ghost festival (Japanese Memorial Day). Families gather, place flowers on the graves of ancestors and loved ones, pray and, of course, eat. With no family or obligations during the holiday, Jiro is free to escape the confines of the *Yushim Seido* and do what his soul cries out to do, explore. With the aid of his now close friend Takeshi, they travel south through *Yedo* toward the bay, and *Yoshiwara*, the floating world of brothels, tearooms and *kabuki*, Japanese theatre.

"Where shall we go during *obon*," Takeshi asks Jiro, although his mind is already made up?

"Well, it's too far for either of us to go home, so that leaves exploration and entertainment. Exploration and entertainment means the sea or *Yoshiwara*. I say we do both," replies Jiro, trying to hide his excitement.

"The sea, of course. Hopefully there will be some breeze, and the sea should help to cool us off. Dining on *yakiika*, grilled squid, *takoyaki*, octopus cakes or fried *kisu*, tempura style small bay fish, sounds great too! Let's get out of here before the goons find some work that requires urgent attention during the holiday. My sentiment exactly. In thirty minutes then?"

"Thirty minutes it is then!"

The two retreat to their respective personal areas, pack a few necessaries in a *furoshiki* and depart via an unfrequented back door.

"We'll find some *onigiri*, plain or garnished rice balls, and some *sembei*, rice crackers along the way," chirps Jiro. "*Ikubei*, let's go (non-standard, Tohoku dialect)!"

The bayshore air is tempered with the smoke of grilling. Vendors with carts and vendors with shacks crowd the area hawking their offerings of squid, octopus, fish, and vegetables, all seasoned, grilled and prepared for the hungry passerby. Tea and *sake* are available to quench the thirst. Neither Jiro nor Takeshi has ever before seen such an offering of prepared foods or such a crowd of diverse people for that matter.

"Let's get some food, then go down by the shore and eat," suggests Jiro.

"Where do we start? There is nothing here that I don't like, and I don't want to spend all my money before we get to *Yoshiwara*," whines Takeshi.

"Let's start with some *yakisakana*, grilled fish of any type, a little *osake*, Japanese rice liquor, and we'll finish the *oniri* that we brought along. A meal fit for my Lord Sumida himself!" boasts Jiro.

The boys enjoy the cool ocean breeze and their late lunch as they plot out their "assault" on *Yoshiwara*. Only after an additional cup of fortitude do they continue their adventure to the floating world of *Yoshiwara*. Gradually the scenery changes from the noisy, vendor-packed bayshore south of the wharfs and warehouses of *Yedo*, to a more serene natural area of surrounding the *Tamagawa* River.

"There it is! Do you see the arch of the bridge above the reeds, Takeshi? That's the bridge over the *Tamagawa* River, the entrance to *Yoshiwara*," exclaims Jiro.

"Before we cross the bridge, we should count our money. How much do you have Jiro," asks Takeshi.

Jiro carefully opens his money bag and counts.

"I have two *isshuban*, Tokugawan silver piece, and three *mon*, Tokugawan bronze coin. How about you Takeshi?"

"About the same. Two *isshuban*, and five *mon*. I wonder if that's enough for a *maiko-san's*, teahouse entertainer, treat?"

"Maybe, but not much of a treat, I suspect," laments Jiro. "Let's go find out!"

Although the streets of the floating world are muddy dirt tracks like everywhere else in Japan, the scent of flowered gardens and the sound of *koto*, traditional Japanese stringed instrument, fill the air. In neat rows, low-walled, gardened compounds surround many of the *chashitsu*, teahouses, and other buildings. Occasionally, a magnificently dressed and coiffured *geisha-san*, traditional female entertainer, in silk kimono and high wooden clogs will cross the street or be visible exiting or entering a building.

"So now what do we do?" whines Takeshi.

"Well, let's go have tea. Choose an establishment, any one. We'll just walk in, sit down, ask for tea and see what happens," decisively decides Jiro.

The boys randomly choose a *chashitsu*, dust themselves off, and enter the gate into its garden. Small lanterns and a stone pathway lead them to the front door. As Jiro slides the door open to the left a beautifully dressed, handsome woman stands discreetly blocking their entrance.

"Good afternoon, **gentlemen**. How may I help you?" she asks.

"We are travelers, and here to refresh ourselves, my lady," spouts Jiro.

"Refresh yourselves? Well, here refreshment comes at a price. Tea ceremony, music, dancing and **refreshment** will cost you one *koban*, Tokugawan gold coin. Do you **young** gentleman carry such a sum? Allow me to answer for you. I think not. So, I **suggest** that you, **gentlemen**, seek your entertainment and **refreshment** elsewhere. Perhaps a snack and some *kabuki* would suit you best. One *mon* will buy you entrance there. Then you can find your ways back to whichever rural well you have sprung and tell all your friends of your **big** day in *Yoshiwara*. When your pockets are a little deeper and your parts are a little bigger, come see me again."

Leaving no room for retort, she turns and walks back into the *chashitsu* leaving the boys standing in the open doorway feeling quite awkward. As they slowly slide the door to the right, closing it softly, they turn and leave.

On the street again, Takeshi turns to Jiro and says, "I actually like her suggestion. Let's go to the theatre, laugh, and save our money. Beside, truthfully, I'm not feeling quite as strong as I was.

Perhaps I'm a little tired from the journey. I'm not sure I could handle a woman like her!"

"Well, I'm certain that they're all not as old and tough as her! Nevertheless, I've never been to *kabuki*. Let's go and see. Perhaps the theatre is not such a bad idea after all. *Ikubei!*"

The disappointment of being neither wealthy nor bold enough to be attractive to even a dried-up old croon is somewhat mitigated by the wonders of *kabuki*. Jiro and Takeshi are well aware that *kabuki* is looked upon with disfavor by officialdom, but it is wildly popular with the masses. Political satire and social commentary, never before part of their consciousness, is introduced to them on a grand scale in the course of two hours that afternoon. They receive a quick course in current events as well as both men's and women's popular fashions, though women have not been a part of *kabuki* for almost two hundred and fifty years. Somewhat to their surprise, the greatest crowed-pleasers, are the actors dressing and playing the roles of women.

"Wow, that is the best *mon* I have ever spent!" exclaims Takeshi.

"Yes, truly. We must come back as soon as possible. I am intrigued. It is as though the *kabuki* has lifted a curtain in my own eyes as well. I feel as though I see things, not the world, but maybe officialdom, differently now. How is that possible after only two hours of a farcical show, Takeshi?"

"I don't know. I feel the same. We must just be tired. Let's find a nice little *minshuku*, lower class inn, take a bath, have something good to eat and sleep until we are satisfied! Then tomorrow we'll see how you feel about the *bakufu*, the *Yushima Seido* and Rector Sokan on the long walk back."

"Good idea. Let's start back in the general direction of central *Yedo*, and keep our eyes peeled for a *minshuku*. I remember seeing several on the way down here. I really need a good, hot bath."

Moving at a comfortably slow pace, the tired boys, still digesting the experiences of the day, locate a small *minshuku*, after only a several *ri* walk. Unlike the proprietor of the *chashitsu*, the innkeeper welcomes them and is happy to accept their silver *isshuban* in return.

Morning comes early and breakfast is served. It is not the institutional breakfast that the boys have now become used to, but a tasty breakfast of good quality steamed rice, grilled fish, pickles, bean paste soup with mushrooms and clams, and fruit. They eat greedily without speaking.

Kaerimichi, the road back, to the *Yushima Seido* is an uneventful, nevertheless a free, half day. Jiro and Takeshi have thoroughly enjoyed their short adventure south of *Yedo*, although their money bags would not have supported a longer one.

On the day following their return to the *Yushima Seido*, Rector Sokan unexpectedly requests their immediate presence in his office. Jiro and Takeshi respond to the rector's summons with some fear and trepidation.

"Someone must have seen us leave or return, don't you think, Jiro?"

"No, we were too careful. More likely, when we didn't show up for meals, someone checked the dormitory and formed a suspicion that we had gone somewhere without authorization. Since it was *obon* and many had either gone home or received authorization to leave the grounds, I don't imagine that our reprimand will be too great."

Takekshi anxiously adds, "I hope you are right!"

Rector Sokan greets the boys with unexpected cordiality. Their attempted serious, straight faces register surprise.

The rector begins, "Ueno Jiro, Nakamori Takeshi, the gods smile on you! The *roju*, one of several senior officials reporting directly to the Shogun, for foreign affairs has requested that our school provide them with two candidates for a special assignment. After careful consideration, I can think of no better candidates representing the *Shohei-zaka Gakumonjo* than you Jiro and you Takeshi. I have not been advised as to what will be required of you. I have only been directed by this higher authority to propose two candidates which are to report to the 'foreign office' tomorrow. Prepare as best you are able, and bring honor to yourselves and the school."

The *Yushima Seido* is only a short distance across *Yedo* from the office of the *roju* responsible for conducting foreign affairs. The somber, protocol-laden atmosphere of the *roju* and the *bakufu* make Jiro and Takeshi feel as though they had departed one world and entered another, and they have.

"Ah, Ueno Jiro, second son of Ueno Takeji, hometown of *Gonohe*, fiefdom of Lord Sumida, your record is without demerit. You seem to have performed adequately in his lordship's stable and at the *Yushima Seido*. You are known to be intelligent with a noteworthy memory. You prefer Geography, Contemporary Affairs and language. You seem to be ambitious and adventurous," flatly states the *roju*. "Are you willing, without reservation, to serve your Shogun for an indeterminate period of time?"

For a moment Jiro stands, eyes averted but fixed on the floor without responding. Then, as if awakening, he straightens, looks up and visually engages the *roju*. "Yes, my lord. I am willing to serve the Shogunate in whatever manner will bring greater glory to the gods and our Emperor, the Son of Heaven."

Momentarily taken back by Jiro's slightly xenophobic but mature answer, the *roju* smiles. Turning his attention to Takeshi, he first reads a litany of observations, then reiterates the same question. Takeshi responds as did Jiro, if only slightly less dramatically.

"Ueno Jiro, Nakamori Takeshi, I will be brief. The Shogunate has recently signed a treaty with the American *gaijin*. The treaty will allow limited trade between Japan and the United States of America. Such trade is not limited to, but will include American-flagged ships using the Japanese ports of *Hakodate* and *Shimoda*. The American *gaijin* presently have a number of naval ships at *Kanagawa*, just south of *Yedo*. They have agreed to allow a small 'delegation' of Japanese to return with them to the United States as observers and apprentices. You are among those chosen to participate on this journey.

"You are to observe everything! Learn their language. Make note of their technology. Take copious notes of their customs and their country. You will be accompanied by Okada-san, a member of my staff. He will see that you are provisioned for the voyage, be responsible for your well-being and your eventual return to Japan. Obey him as you would me. Be aware that these *gaijin* are untrustworthy and unpredictable. The voyage may be long and dangerous. Serve well and you will find position and reward upon your return to Japan.

"I have written instructions in this letter which you are to present to Rector Sokan immediately upon your return to school. He will, of course, help prepare you for the journey. Return here tomorrow after your mid-day meal. Okada-san will be waiting with *jinrikusha*, one or two person taxi pulled by a man, and porters to bring you to *Kanagawa*. The American commander, Admiral Perry and his officers are expecting you aboard his ship *Susquehanna*. May your work be pleasing to the gods and to His Imperial Majesty. Now go!"

Chapter Seven
Ketch of the Day

David is faced with a great dilemma. Does he tell his father and mother about his great find? Does he risk having his father make inquiries into the loss of a ketch and possibly discover its rightful owner? Sharing his secret with any of his friends would be the surest way to spread the news about town and no doubt result in the loss of his prize. He will require help to claim, salvage and restore the boat, but help from whom and when. After only short self-deliberation he comes to the only decision he could have made. He will do as John Paul Jones would have done; he will go straight at 'em, and cross the T. He begins to formulate a plan.

David "attacks" the most difficult obstacle first, his father. "Father, I need your advice and counsel on a matter of great importance to me."

"Advice and counsel on a matter of great importance to you? You're a little young to be shipping out or marrying aren't you, Davie?"

"Yes, of course, Father. I didn't mean to be so, stiff, so formal, but this really is important to me. I need your advice and possibly your help."

"Yes, yes, certainly, Davie. What is on your mind, boy?"

David explains, "On Saturday, while fishing in the bay, I, by chance, came across a seemingly abandoned, swamped boat. I believe it to be a ketch, it has two masts? It appears to have been there for some time, but I'm not sure. I think it can be salvaged, Father. I'd like to claim it and try!"

"Interesting. Yes, help is what you'll need. You may have come across something with your discovery. But it's not only help you will need, it is money and time as well. Are you up to such a large undertaking, David?"

"I believe so, Father. I do have a plan. First, if you would contact the sheriff and make 'our' claim to the boat. You had suggested an apprenticeship with Mr. MacDonald at the newspaper. I will write to Mr. MacDonald and inquire about a job after school. I'll need some money to restore the boat. If'n I can work for Mr. MacDonald during the week, I can spend some time on the boat, after chores, on Saturday. What do you think, Father?"

"I think you have a good, clear plan of action. I have doubts about the feasibility of the salvage, but if you want to try, I will support your effort."

David tries to temper his excitement in front of his father. Adults seem to prefer quiet, dutiful children rather than those who express themselves freely. He has learned to refrain from expressing himself freely. David retreats from his father's presence, and goes to write his letter to Mr. MacDonald the newspaperman.

Dear Mr. MacDonald,

My name is David McDougal. I believe you know my father. Presently, I attend school at Miss Madson's Normal School in Leonardstown. My father has advised me that you are considering taking on an apprentice. Although I am not yet graduated from the 8ᵗʰ grade, I am willing to work on an occasional basis, as you may have various tasks with which you need help. I am available most days after school and on Saturdays as you may require. As for my payment, I propose $.15 per day and the opportunity to learn the newspaper business.

Thank you for your consideration of my proposal.

Sincerely,
David McDougal

His die cast, David waits for the result of the sheriff's inquiry and his proposal to Mr. McDonald. In the meantime, David checks the foundered boat daily as if protecting a staked claim.

In the course of the next several weeks, the replies David has been waiting for arrive. First, Mr. MacDonald, proprietor and editor in chief of the Leonardstown *Democrat Observer*, writes David accepting his offer of occasional employment at a generous $.05 per hour, slightly better than half the current adult common laborer rate. His employment can be effective immediately. About two weeks later, the County Sheriff advises David's father that, since the boat bears no name, no known owner of the boat can be located nor has the sheriff received a report of any similar boat being lost of recent, the boat is his to claim. It may have been a rum runner. David may claim the hulk and begin his salvage operation.

After a seeming eternity of waiting, the big day has finally arrived. This Saturday, after dinner, he will take the first step in salvaging his boat. David's friend Nathan and his team of big, black Percherons will assist in pulling the boat out of the reeds.

"Nathan, it'll be low tide about two-thirty. Right after dinner you can drive your blacks down to the shore, then we'll let'm graze awhile while we bail 'er out. Once we got the water out, we'll hook 'er up to the team and pull 'er out. I put a pry under the bow and try to lift 'er just a bit out of the muck. It'll be the easiest four bits you ever made!"

"Do you really think it will work, Davie? It's a not a small boat, and she's worked into the muck pretty good. True, the bailing will lighten 'er up, but I don't want to hurt the blacks. My dad would never forgive me."

"Oh, for Christ's sake, Nathan, you've already got one of the blacks with a strained hock. It'll work, I know it will. The trick is, we must get the prow of the boat up out of the muck and clear. Then she'll pull right up on to beach. Then you unfasten the tugs, and we'll roll 'er over onto one side and I can begin to clean 'er up."

"All right, Davie. I sure hope this works. It is doesn't I'm going to be grounded for a very long time."

For the better part of an hour, David and Nathan bail out the water and clean debris from the boat, while the blacks graze not far away. After they have bailed out as much as practical, David wedges one of the boat's booms under the prow as Nathan jumps up, straddles the end of the lever adding his full body weight as and David pulls down in an effort to ease the prow out of its resting place in the muck.

"It's no use, Davie. She won't budge. What do we do now?"

"It'll work. We just need a better leverage point, a fulcrum. Let's find a big rock. We'll roll it down into a position along the side of the boat parallel to the bow. We'll wedge the boom underneath and try again."

With maximum effort the boys manage to coax the bow of the boat out of the sticky bottom. As David maintains pressure on the lever, Nathan grabs a bailing bucket, scoops up rocky fill from higher up on the beach and pours the fill under the forward hull of the boat. Nathan repeats the process a half dozen times until he is fairly certain that the boat won't just return to its place in the muck once David releases the lever.

"All right, Davie, let 'er down easy. I think that fill will keep 'er up out of the muck. That's it. That's it. Good! That is as good as we can hope for. Let's give 'er a tug and see what happens."

"Nathan, attach the double tree to the anchor chain. That will give us good solid pulling points on both the team and boat sides. Here we go!"

"Yaah! Get up there, Fred! Get up there, Barney! Pull boys, pull! Pull that bitch out of the bay!"

Muscles flexing, sinews taunt, necks arched, the big, black Percherons leap into the pull as only a well-trained team knows how. The tugs tighten seconds after Nathan snaps the lines on their rumps and barks encouragement. The double tree equalizes the pull on the anchor chain. The ketch, bow now resting on Nathan's gravel fill, and the hull emptied of excess water weight, inches forward, hesitantly at first, then begins to slide more quickly as its prow comes up onto the beach and out of the confines of the reeds and muck.

"Yaah, yaah! Keep up the pull, Fred. Keep up the pull, Barney. Yaah!"

As the midship clears the water and the full hull slides up onto the beach, the forward momentum slows and then suddenly stops. "Whoa boys, whoa!" commands Nathan. For the moment the blacks can do no more other than scratch deeper ruts in the gravelly soil.

"That's 'bout it, Davie. I don't think Fred and Barney can do no more."

"No, that's great Nathan. Your team did their job and got the boat up onto the shore. Let 'em graze a little more and come help me lever 'er over onto 'er starboard side. Later, after she dries off, I'll start by scraping 'er clean on the port side and see where we're at. Oh, by the way, here's your four bits. You, Fred and Barney earned 'em today!"

With school out for the summer, after morning chores David hurries to Leonardstown where he spends five to six hours with Mr. MacDonald at the newspaper office. Mundane tasks at first; sweeping, and cleaning the glass-pane windows, these duties gradually change to include supply inventory, type-setting and even printing. Armed with an inquiring mind and keen observation, David quickly learns the power of the pen.

On occasion David glimpses another in Mr. MacDonald household employ. A shy young Negress named Nelly can sometimes be seen preparing, setting a table or cleaning the house. She may be David's age or a little older, he cannot tell, **they** all look the same to him. Her race notwithstanding, he is intrigued by her simplicity and freshness. He tries to learn more about her but is somewhat brusquely rebuffed by Mr. MacDonald when he dares to ask a question concerning her presence in the household.

One day while retrieving some ink from the supply room, David sees Nelly out behind the house peeling vegetables for dinner. He tentatively approaches her. He's never spoken to a Negress before, or a Negro for that matter.

"Good morning, miss, what is your name?" inquires David in a friendly but tentative manner.

"My name is Nelly, Young Sir, but don't you be talking to me or Master MacDonald goin' be very angry. I don'ts want no trouble with the master."

"But I'm David, I work for Mr. MacDonald too. Surely he wouldn't be angry if we talked a little?"

"I don't really work **for** Master MacDonald, I just works. Theys call me Nelly, and it don't matter who you be, I ain't supposed to talk to you."

"All right, Nelly, I won't talk to you today, but I'll see you again sometime and maybe we can talk then? Good day, Miss Nelly."

David turns and returns to the printing office. Nelly, instead of disappearing into the unseen recesses of the MacDonald home, just stands there with her mouth slightly open. No one has ever really wanted to know her name before. No one has really ever wanted to talk with her before. And no one has really ever spoken pleasantly and politely to her before, certainly no white boy. Nelly is puzzled by her encounter with David. Reality however quick reasserts itself into her consciousness, she abandons her peeling and retreats to the kitchen.

That night, lying in bed, David's thoughts return, uncharacteristically, not to his salvage operation by the bay but to little Nelly standing out behind the newspaper office. His eyes closed, he recalls the bow in her hair, not a pink satin bow like the girls at school, but a simple pattern bow, looking like it was cut from an old dress. The memory of his eyes follows her lines down past the white smile accentuated by her very dark skin, along her neck to her half exposed shoulders where her loose fitting dress begins. His eye's journey continues to her erect nipples pushing out from beneath their cover, to her hips swaying back and forth and she stands there nervously half listening to his introduction and half scanning the background for Mr. MacDonald to suddenly emerge from the newspaper office. His journey stops at her bare feet then follows her lines back again to the dark, black pools which are her eyes. She is ordinary, yet the image imprinted in his mind is sensual, extraordinary. David's unrealized erection suddenly releases itself into his drawers. *Wow, what just happened?* David has had erections before but never like that. Why? Usually his involuntary erections just throb, leaving him frustrated and unsatisfied. A little surprised but at the same relieved, David, now embarrassed with himself, removes his stained drawers and stashes them beneath his bed. He crawls back into bed and tries to focus again on Nelly. David's mind, however, has already left her far behind as it tries to lead him back to the freshly scraped hull planks of his ketch. Dreamlessly, he falls asleep, his body at least, already preparing for another eventful day.

David's salvage project consumes all of his time not already committed to either farm chores, the newspaper office or his family. His earnings from the newspaper office job have helped with his salvage expenses, yet he is already taken one advance of ten dollars from Mr. MacDonald and a loan of another twenty dollars from his father.

After scraping the port hull, David carefully inspects the planks for rot or warpage, and, most importantly, the seams between the planks. He probes with a chalking iron suspect seams, and repairs them when necessary with cotton chalk and oakum. Satisfied with his work, all the seams are then resealed with pitch, after which he applies paint. A work in progress becomes a school in progress in the art of marine repair. Nathan, too busy with farm chores and having even less marine repair knowledge than David, is replaced by Henry, a retired gentleman no longer young. Among his other skills, Henry has spent some years in a boatyard near Annapolis, he has become David's mentor in all things nautical.

The better part of the summer has been consumed in the refinishing of the port side of the ketch. With just weeks remaining before the start of school, less discretionary time and changing weather, the ketch is rolled over on its refinished port side exposing the starboard to the same routine. Much to David's delight, with knowledge gleaned from Henry, experience gained on refinishing the port side, and, of course, Henry's helping hand, progress on the starboard side proceeds considerably faster than it had on the port side. Before summer's end, both sides of the hull, as well as the rear transom, have been refinished. "Ketch of the Day" is not yet ready to sail, but she could be refloated. The summer of his thirteenth year has been a summer to remember. The ketch will be "winterized" as time permits and left until spring. David tries inconspicuously to look out for Nelly when at the newspaper office now only on Saturday mornings, but has only, on occasion, seen her shadow, or what he assumes to be her shadow moving about the house. In his observations he does make note of an outside latch on her quarters. Odd for city or town help, she does not live in the house she serves. In his mind he keeps going back to the latch, wondering why? David doesn't particularly look forward to school, but considers the possibility of procuring mail order books from the library in Annapolis with the help of Miss Madson, books on subjects of his own choosing and interests. Life in his thirteenth year is full of possibilities.

Chapter Eight
The Tokaido Road

*I*t is over one thousand *ri* from *Hagi* Castle to *Yedo*, the seat of power of the Tokugawa Shogunate and home of the *Yushima Seido*. Young Takachika expects his journey to take about twenty-eight days barring incidents, bad weather or just bad josh. The first days out on the road are pleasant. The Mori entourage travels comfortably in good weather and in the knowledge that they remain within the *Choshu* Domain and relative safety. The main east-west road extends east from *Hagi* Castle, first leading slightly north to *Ikaki*, then turning slightly south to *Aki* and then direct to *Okayama* Castle, the group's first intermediate stop.

Okayama Castle, one of the most beautiful and powerful castles in the region is controlled by the Ikeda *han* of the *Himeji* Domain. There, in the midst of the military might of the Ikeda *han* and under the controlling watch of agents and customs officials of the *bakufu*, the *Kuen*, modern *Korakuen*, gardens stand out as an island of tranquility and peace along the banks of the *Aashi*

River. The gardens are one of three scenic promenades in Japan, cultural masterpieces worthy of time spent there. Takachika plans to stroll the gardens and pay due respect to the Ikeda *han*.

As the east-west road approaches *Okayama*, the road widens and is better maintained. Peasant villages, inns and travelers become more numerous here. Jedo, the assassin, and his gang take advantage of the less-populated, lawless region just outside *Okayama* and the Ikeda sphere of influence, in *Aki*. Here the undergrowth along the road is heavier, forests thicker and darker, and far fewer travelers populate the way. Classically, on a bend in the road, Jedo prepares an ambuscade. A local hireling will move slowly along the road with an obstructive load. As the Mori entourage slows to evaluate, then move past the decoy, Jedo and two picked men will emerge from the undergrowth and engage the party.

Jedo outlines his plan to his "picked" men. "Our local hire will distract them, first with his load then with his knife. We will emerge from the bush on the north side of the road. Kon, you will hamstring the rear pack animal with your sword. The noise and thrashing of animal will draw some of their attention away from the hireling and confuse them. Slaughter the servants as you like but young Takachika is not to be touched and is to be allowed to run for home. Sadly, our hireling will also die in the melee. I will recover the *koban* he demanded for his services as well as Takachika's money box. After we have chased our young lordling back down the road for a *ri* or two, we will retire to *Okayama* and enjoy the pleasures of a teahouse until we are recalled. Do you two understand? My Lord Mori will tolerate no mistakes!"

"We got it. What could be easier? Cut a mule, slit a throat and scare a boy," replies Kon.

"Easy maybe, but don't get careless in your work. This job is for hire not for pleasure! We are to appear desperate and reckless, in order to confuse young Takachika and any authorities who may want to poke their noses into this 'wanton' act. Got it, Kon?" asks Jedo in a slightly threatening manner.

"Yeah, yeah. Don't get excited," snips Kon.

"Now get ready. I'll reconnoiter west and see where they're at. I should be back soon. No loud talking or drinking! And don't allow yourselves to be seen!" commands Jedo.

With his basic plan set, location well chosen, and men in place, Jedo slowly walks west seeking out the Mori entourage. He doesn't have to go far before he first hears then sights the entourage moving steadily, if slowly, up the road. Jedo waits in the bush as they come into sight.

"*Kuso*, shit, other travelers have attached themselves to the lordling like barnacles to a ship. We can certainly dispatch them to the gods as well, but it makes for a messier operation. The authorities will surely investigate. More booty perhaps, but we'll have to spend time eliminating sign of our presence and keep a low profile in the teahouses of *Okayama*," mumbles Jedo to himself.

The little entourage continues moving east toward *Okayama* oblivious to sudden death awaiting them only several *ri* up the road. Some peasants carrying goods to market in *Okayama* have attached themselves to young Takachika's train. They gossip amongst themselves, eat *onigi*, rice balls stuffed with salted fish, or pickles and wrapped in seaweed, plain or roasted, and laugh, feeling secure "in the entourage" of the son of powerful Lord Mori, Prince of *Nagato* and *daimyo* of the *Choshu* Domain.

Takachika rides a beautiful bay charger at the front of the diverse group. He too feels better with the peasants in tow. The larger the group, the more secure and important Takachika feels as he looks down to the left, then to the right and up the road toward *Okayama*. As the entourage comes around a sharp bend in the road he sees another peasant traveler trying to balance a heavy load. As he comes closer, the absurdity of the scene irritates him greatly.

"*Bakaero*, imbecile, move out of the middle of the road. Let us pass. What kind of idiot obstructs the entire road with his load?" yells young Takachika at the peasant.

"Yes, my lord. Right away my lord," answers the peasant without ever looking up or back.

Suddenly Takachika feels a shiver go up his spine. How does this peasant know I'm a "lord" without ever looking at me? And why **is** he so clumsily obstructing the road. Takachika instinctively reaches down for the *tanto* hidden beneath his saddle bags. As his left hand touches the hilt of the knife, he hears confused hollering and the high-pitched screams of one of the pack animals. Jedo has struck his flank.

Takachika, half-turned to the left in his saddle with *tanto* in hand, sees one of the pack animals shed his load in frenzied bucking and go running and kicking into the brush. He identifies three men attacking the entourage. One peasant is already on the ground curled-up holding his gut. The other peasants have dropped their baggage and are running back down the road in the opposite direction. Takachika's retainers rush onto either side of him as if to protect him. One, Sadao, his *Kendo* master, pulls out a bamboo *shinai* with which he hopes to fend off one or more of the attackers.

The hireling, unaware of the Takachika's *tanto*, grabs for the reins of the charger. Young and flexible, reins in his right hand and *tanto* in his left, Takachika thrusts the dagger straight into the hireling's left eye. The hireling's hand melts off the reins, clutching the socket where his left eye used to dwell, oozing goo and spurting blood as he falls back flat on his ass. The peasants have fled with the exception of one, now dead on the road, as have both of his pack animals. Sadao stands, bamboo "sword" in hand, at the ready in a defensive poise to repel the three remaining attackers. Toshiya, the lordling's tutor clutches a rock picked-up off the road next to the charger's rear. Takachika turns his charger and faces the attackers along with Sadao. Toshiya, now in the rear, previously the front of the party holds his rock while scanning the road for more.

Kon, suddenly raises his *katana* above his head and charges Sadao. Sadao deftly sidesteps the attacker and swings his *shinai* hard against the back brainstem of Kon's head. The impact of the *shinai* is exaggerated by the loud sound of the snap of the "sword." Kon goes sprawling on the ground. At the same time Takachika reins his charger back and then up on its hind legs, stomping down hard on Kon's back and neck. In the heat of the moment Takachika cannot determine whether the attacker is dead or not, but certainly he is no longer a participant in this exchange.

Momentarily, Jedo is dumbfounded. He has lost half of his "attack force" and has only one dumb peasant and a wounded pack animal to show for it. He changes tactics. He whispers to his man.

"I will feign an attack on the lordling. His retainer with the *shinai* will try to fend me off, you take him from the back when he engages me. Now!"

Both assassins raise their *katana* and rush the remaining entourage. As expected, Sadao turns to protect the lordling, but unexpectedly Takachika spurs his charger forward at a gallop, colliding with Jedo head-on. Sadao then engages the remaining assassin with all his *Kendo* skill. Momentarily, Jedo lies half-unconscious on the ground, the breath knocked out of him from his collision with the charger. Before Takachika can turn his charger for another attack on Jedo, Toshiya picks up a large rock from along the margins of the road and drops it onto Jedo's skull. A dull thud and a sickening crack bring Jedo's service to Lord Mori to an end. Alone, and knowing surrender not to be an option, the remaining assassin follows the route of the wounded pack animal and runs for the brush. The attack has failed; it is over.

Young Takachika unemotionally reassesses his situation. His pack animals have fled leaving part or all of their loads scattered along the road and in the forest brush. Even if recovered, at least one of the animals is wounded. The peasants who fled the scene, if located, cannot be counted on to support his version of the attack. They will twist their stories to whichever angle benefits them the most. Although he and his retainers are unharmed and should he report the attack to the authorities in *Okayama*, surely he and they will be held until an investigation is complete. Young Takachika makes the easy decision to abandon the journey, return to *Hagi* Castle, and seek the counsel of Takahashi and his father.

"We must return to *Hagi* Castle, Takachika announces to his retainers. "We have lost our supplies and most of our money. I do not believe this brigandry to be random. This is treachery. Salvage what we can. We are heading home."

Relieved that the journey has been prematurely terminated, the retainers quickly gather those items strewn about. Within the hour they have reassembled their packs and are headed west at a quick pace.

After four days and three nights the now ragged entourage reenters the gates of *Hagi* Castle. Those who see young Takachika and his retainers enter, try not to stare or let their faces betray their shock and disbelief. Takachika wastes no time in seeking an audience with his father and Counselor Takahashi.

"Father, the brigands first blocked the road ahead, then came at us from out of the wood. We had no weapons or armor but defended ourselves the best we could," blurts Takachika before the first question is asked.

"*Ah so desu ka,*" ah, yes see, replies Lord Mori in a softer than usual voice, looking straight at young Takachika without regard to Counselor Takahashi seated nearby.

"The gift is safe, Father. I carried it with me on my mount. The money box was recovered along with most of our supplies. We were unable to find one of the pack animals and the other was too badly wounded to make the journey home. We left the wounded animal along with the unnecessary and inexpensive items by the side of the road. I did not contact the authorities," reports Takachika.

"Good. You did well son," compliments Lord Mori.

"Father, I do not believe this assault was random."

"Oh. Why do you say that?" queries Lord Mori.

"Because one of the brigands, the one blocking the road addressed me as, my lord without even looking at me. It was as though he was expecting us."

"I see. You possess good deductive reasoning, my son. But who would you suspect?" asks Lord Mori.

"The *bakufu*, Father. I suspect the authorities themselves were trying to kill me, the son of you, my lord. In this way the line of inheritance of the Mori *han* would be weakened. Our domain would be at risk. The *bakufu* benefit from our weakened state," answers Takachika with some confidence.

"Yes, that is possible. I follow your train of thought. It is possible," agrees Lord Mori. "Takahashi, what do you think?"

"Yes, my lord. I agree with young Takachika. That scenario is a distinct possibility. The *bakufu* hire some unemployed rogues to do their dirty work, 'paying' them with our own money stolen in the attack."

"I will never forget this lesson father. The *bakufu*, the Shogun himself, they are our enemies. I will never do homage. I will never submit to them until death unites me with our ancestors and the gods!"

Lord Mori glances at Counselor Takahashi and smiles.

Chapter Nine
University Man

*I*t was natural and expected that Robert would someday become a "university man," but none had imagined an Acceptance Letter shortly after he sixteenth birthday.

Master Robert H. Pruyn
Albany, New York

Dear Master Pruyn,
We are pleased to announce your acceptance to Rutgers
College for the academic year 1831-32.

A general reception and orientation will be held at
Alexander Johnson Hall at 1:00 P.M. on Saturday 7
September 1831. We will be pleased provide you with
additional information on curriculum, residency and so-
cieties at that time.

On behalf of the regents, administration and faculty of Rutgers College, we congratulate you and look forward to making a personal acquaintance at that time.

Johannes S. VanHeusen, President

The People's Line steamships ply the Hudson River from Albany to New York City. The populist-ring to the name of the company is Daniel Drew's, proprietor, answer to the "common man" trend of Jacksonian America. Cornelius "Commodore" Vanderbilt operates the competing North River Lines, but has secretly partnered with Peoples Line operator Daniel Drew in order to limit competitive fares, so in effect, The People's Line is no less "of the people, by the people and for the people" as is that owned by millionaire financier Mr. Vanderbilt.

On a beautiful end of summer day, Robert with travel trunk packed for the school year stands on the pier as the steamer Mohawk prepares to embark its New York bound passengers. Robert, though the son of a prominent and wealthy family, holds a second class ticket, consistent with his family's conservative financial views and its abhorrence to the idea of flaunting one's wealth. Freshly barbered and wearing a handsome brown woolen suit he awaits the steam whistle blast which will signal that the ship is ready to embark passengers.

The five-mile-per-hour transit from Albany to New York City is scheduled for thirty-six hours of wood-burning, paddle-churning and sight-seeing along the beautiful Hudson River Valley. Too early for fall colors, one of the many highlights of the trip for Robert is steaming by the imposing West Point fortress, site of

Benedict Arnold's betrayal of United States and since its founding in 1807 by Colonel Sylvanus Thayer, home of the United States Military Academy. Robert had given some thought to a martial education, but thinks better of it and wishes to pursue his passion for letters, business and the law. Rutgers College will better afford him these opportunities.

Time passes quickly on Robert's first journey alone. He arrives in New York on the north side of the Hudson River. He must now find boarding for the night and arrange his transit across the Hudson to New Jersey and on to New Brunswick, where his student life will begin. Finding suitable accommodation for the night, Robert proceeds next day to New Brunswick. He has chosen the Paulus Hook Ferry, embarking at Cortlandt Street on the Manhattan side and discharging him at Paulus Hook, New Jersey. From there he can proceed on the Camden and Amboy Railroad direct to New Brunswick. Costing one dollar fifty cents, but within his budgeted travel allowance, Robert is the first in his extended family to ride on steam-powered railroad conveyance. Thoroughly impressed with his ride on the railroad, he arrives at Rutgers College, New Brunswick, New Jersey, on Friday September 6, 1832 only sixty-three hours after departing Albany.

Somewhat to Robert's dismay, his new curriculum does not greatly differ from that of Albany Academy. His father's admonitions still ringing in his ears, he continues his studies in Latin, Greek, Rhetoric, Mathematics and Physics. He is, however, allowed some latitude in Music, and a newly accepted field of Natural Science. Not unlike Albany Academy, the trending "common school" philosophy is present here, as is emphasis on citizenship and morality, important groundwork for a fledgling nation. Robert finds distraction in college societies. Typical of American families of Dutch heritage, the Pruyns have always been mindful of theirs and other faiths but are not overly religious people. He is quick to become a member of the Rhetoric Society, but avoids debating popular sensational or religious affairs, preferring instead to focus on a more Hamiltonian Federalist agenda of national importance and public policy. His favorite trick when preparing for debate is to liberally sprinkle slightly out of context Supreme Court opinions into his arguments. His overawed opponents often concede a point in question before realizing that they have simply been out-foxed not out-debated.

The library is Robert's refuge. Here without pressure or prejudice, Robert may retreat into some obscure point of law, delve into Taoist thought, read a dictionary in order to fortify his vocabulary, or simply stare out the window onto the graceful grounds of the college and daydream of a future as an attorney at law or key public servant.

"Hey, Bobbie, there is a traveling theatre group in town. Some of us are going to flee the grounds and enjoy some Royall Tyler comic offering. 'The Contrast' is to be played. I suspect it will be good. Will you join us?" asks Robert's friend Andre.

The theatre group has taken up temporary residence in a pre-Revolutionary War, wood-frame structure which has clearly seen its best days a decade or two before. It may once have served as a livery, the fragrance remains half-sealed in its wooden beams. Fortified with a supply of liquor of unknown origin, the university men sit in the shadows drinking, gossiping and trying not to be recognized by any townspeople associated with the college as the once-popular play drones on without as much comedy as was expected. The only genuine amusement, is a strawberry-blond haired actress, both too old and too experienced for a young university man like Robert. Ignoring his friend's antics, Robert engrosses himself in the motions and the dialog of the actress there in front of him.

"Robert, what in hades? You didn't answer the question. Are you or are you not going to stay at college during the Christmas holiday? Oh, forgive me! I see, it's the girl. Our dear Robert here has discovered the sin of lust. But the question is, just how far is he willing to pursue his new found feeling before he spooks and retreats back into his library sanctuary?" teases Andre.

"Get thee behind me, Satan!" responds Robert. Whether directing his retort to Andre or toward himself remains unclear to all.

"So I'm the Satan then, Bobbie? Naughty Andre, having lured you off grounds and 'forced' you to drink all that demon rum. I take exception to your accusation," jokingly jousts Andre while offering up another swig of the bottle. "I have merely plucked the sty from thy eye in order you may see. I, along with my good fellows here, have merely lifted the curtain from around your dark and sheltered life. It is **you**, not I that desires to lift the skirt of fair yon maiden. Although I submit to you, that fair yon maiden is neither so fair, and certainly not the maiden that she may appear in your mind's eye," expounds Andre in his most taunting manner.

"Will you be quiet, Andre? Maybe it is you that should take the stage and let the girl come sit next to me. Her company could not be any less desirable, and I am certain her whoring must pale by comparison to yours! Now, if you please!" responds Robert, trying to salvage a measure of pride in front of the other fellows.

Andre, emboldened by measures of ill-gotten Bahaman rum, is not so easily cowed. He continues to have fun with Robert. "If it isn't Alonso Quijana, the country gentleman gazing longingly at his Dulcinea. Oh, Dulcinea, Dulcinea."

In front of the fellows, Robert can do nothing more than persevere.

Finally, Robert and the fellows return to their dormitory long before day's light, and are, as far as they can discern, free of suspicion. Many more such escapades mar their veneer of propriety in the next four years, one as equally debauch as the next. The College, on the occasions of Harvest and Spring festivals, organizes events with socially suitable young ladies. Robert shows little or no enthusiasm in New Jersey social life, however, longing to return to Albany and his life's work.

In their years at Rutgers College, Robert, Andre and the fellows form bonds of friendship that, though tested in the coming conflagration, remain a lifetime. Before graduation in the spring of 1835, Robert receives the letter from home which has been waiting for since arriving here three years ago.

Dear Son,

We are anxiously anticipating your imminent graduation from Rutgers College. Your mother and I could not be more proud of your achievements there.

You will be pleased to be informed that Mr. Erasumus Vanderhornt, Esq. has agreed to place you as an appren-

tice at law upon your return to Albany. With application and hard work, he feels that you may examine for the bar within three years. We hope that these arrangements meet with your approval.

May the Lord keep you safe in your journey. We will expect you in July.

With our love,

Baccularium atrium, Bachelor of Arts, degree in hand, Robert repacks his by now dusty travel trunk for the return trip to Albany. He so looks forward to the riding the Camden and Amboy railroad again and now three years removed from his father's penny-saving ways that he purchases a First Class ticket in order to enjoy the ride in style. In New Brunswick, Robert boards the First Class carriage. The interior is richly adorned with comfortable leather seats, wool carpet, polished wood and brass fixtures. He doesn't feel out of place, only slightly self-conscious having spent the additional dollar. At a top speed of thirty miles per hour, Robert is lulled to sleep by the passing pastoral scenery and the rhythmic clatter of the iron-covered rails. Having only just fallen off to sleep, his dream is suddenly shattered by the reality of a hard impact against the wooden floor. An iron rail crystallized then broken under the pressure of the passing locomotive and tender raises up from the railbed, perforating the floor vertically, then ripping its way down the carriage floor horizontally, taking all that is before it. Floor boards, carpet, seats, bruised and broken bodies are all heaped up and pulled to the rear of the carriage until the forward momentum of the train is spent. Robert is aghast at the carnage. He has read newspaper accounts of these so-called snake's head broken rails before. The Camden and Amboy Line rails are actually longitudinal wood rails covered by iron rail strap. Here and on other lines, the iron straps are prone to breakage under extreme weather or stress, causing, in some instances, severe damage and injury, as Robert's First Class carriage and passengers experience today.

After some delay, the passengers are transported to the next C and A station from which they continue their respective journeys the following day.

On July 3, 1835 Robert returns to Albany aboard the People's Line steamer *Mohawk*. Pier side he is enthusiastically greeted by his extended family, congratulated and welcomed home. Tomorrow is the Fourth of July. Albany, like most American cities, towns and villages will celebrate the nation's fifty-ninth birthday. The day after, Robert will start his career in law.

Chapter Ten
The Dreaming Tree

Chizuru floats timelessly in her mind. She hears murmurs, but does not answer. She feels hot, then senses cool dampness on her forehead, limbs and torso. She dreams like she has never dreamed before. Some of the dreams are nonsensical, others colorful, but she always returns to a road. Effortlessly she walks down this road, a road shadowed by large Cedar trees. *Ishidouro*, carved stone lanterns, in pairs, stand intermittent along the way. There is light, yet no sunshine. She hears water running and her throat is dry. She is drawn, almost a yearning to move forward. A shrine, or what she believes to be a shrine, somewhere along this road. She cannot see this shrine, but she knows it is there. She asks herself, "Where am I going? Am I dying? Am I dead?" Her question goes unanswered as she continues down the road.

Voices, no *a* voice, small and almost indiscernible speaks. "I am whom your heart desires. I created thee. I am part of thee. You are not whole without me. I am not whole without you. I am

the *kami*, spirit, inside of you. Your *kami* is part of me. Never forget this moment, my revelation to thee. Though the road is long, you will come back to me. You will never forsake me nor I forsake you. I love thee, Amen"

When Chizuru opens her eyes she sees a pale young man half-seated, half-bending over her. She does not know him, yet she feels no fear. His pale blue eyes, light skin and hair betray his race; he is not of Japan. He speaks, but not directly to her. She hears the word, "Amen."

Closing her eyes, she repeats the word in her mind, "Amen." What does this word mean? Where has she hear it before? She is tired. She sleeps again.

One morning, several days later, Chizuru opens her eyes, scans the room, empty of people and feels the urge to get up. She lifts her head, pushes aside the *kakebuton*, futon cover, and slowly rises to a sitting position. She rests. After a moment or two, first on her knees then on her feet, she stands. It feels good to stand, stretch and be alive again. Slightly off-balance, darkness descending, she faints and falls in a heap upon her futon. The low decibel thump and vibration on the Pine board floors brings the young doctor and her mother running back into her room.

"Chizuru, Chizuru, what are you doing? Did you try to stand? Why didn't you call for help?" her mother asks in a concerned manner.

"There, there, girl. Rest. Don't worry, Mother, she'll be all right now. She is just weak from the disease," says the young doctor in a reassuring manner. As if suddenly realizing that no one in this room, house or village understands a word of Dutch, he changes to most rudimentary, but understandable Japanese. "*Daijobu desu. Shimpai shinai de kudasai,* she's all right. Don't worry please."

Kneeling beside her, the young doctor assists her in standing. It is at this moment that she feels the light chain and simple cross around her neck. Her eyes glance down at the cross, then back to the foreigner. He affirms the gift with his eyes, and touches his heart as if to express its significance to him. He makes the sign of the cross and says, "Amen." Chizuru makes the connection. The necklace, the likes of which she has never owned, represents this foreigner's *kami.* This *kami* spoke to her. She remembers. She remembers "her" *kami* using the same word, "Amen."

Chizuru has had her epiphany. Now, standing in her room, before her birth mother, facing this foreigner she makes the mental connection of one eternal and universal God. A God present in her, in her mother, in him, a foreigner "from across the waters," a land half a world away. This God of the Cross has saved her, will not forsake her, and loves her. She has purpose in this life, now she must find it. Amen.

Chizuru does not share her dreams with anyone. She keeps these secret, folded into her heart, invisible to others. So too does she keep the doctor's gift, always there near her heart, hidden in her layered kimono. Since the "dreaming time," she has changed. Changed, not in a physical way, or even an emotional way, she is still an adolescent young girl. Rather, Chizuru has changed in a spiritual way, the only possible outcome really, her soul having encountered the universal spirit and its message of purpose, love and hope.

Chizuru's father, Yoshio, swaggering about the village in officialdom, concerned primarily about his *bakufu* overseers and his pride, does not notice the change. He is relieved that his only daughter did not die of the disease. He too has a secret now. He must bury his appeal to and harboring of the young foreign doctor. He knowingly and willingly violated the Shogun's Separation Edict for his own purpose. If found out, humiliation and *bakin*, fine, would probably be the best he could expect. A *koban* or two to the Shogun's coffers would not alter his larger ambitions, but loss of his official position would. Yoshio has, since Chizuru's birth, planned to offer up his beautiful daughter into an arranged marriage with local nobility. This plan remains unaltered. His machinations in this effort have, in fact, only accelerated. Now, more than ever, he fears losing Chizuru to accident, injury or illness before he can safely marry her off, thereby elevating his social status forever. Death or scandal, either would ruin his plans forever.

Mothers seem to have an extrasensory ability to divine change. Chizuru's mother is no exception to this general rule. She notices in Chizuru what she believes, at first, to be residual effects of the disease, an aura of quiet slowness about her. Later she notices how Chizuru applies herself to even mundane tasks. She seems to have purpose. Chizuru's mother ponders these observations even as her father conspires tirelessly to his own ends.

The powerful Mori *han* lays claim to lands on both the north and south shores of the *Shimonoseki Straits*. *Nagasaki* and nearby *Shikimi*, are part of the Ryozuji *han* Domain but heavily influenced by its larger, northern neighbor. Although officially a functionary of the *bakufu*, Yoshio is loosely subordinated to the Ryozuji *han* in whose fiefdom he lives. Fishing in deeper waters, however, Yoshio has let it be known that his beautiful and talented daughter Chizuru is available for marriage to eligible parties of either the Ryozuji or Mori *han*. He baits the offer with a handsome dowry and knowledge that he, as a *bakufu* functionary, could potentially serve as a backdoor conduit to the *ryoju* in *Yedo* .

Having temporarily thwarted the *bakufu* at their favorite game, hostage taking, Lord Mori, seeking a backdoor channel to *Yedo*, takes the bait offered by Yoshio. He will seek Chizuru as a bride for Takachika. From his vantage point, a marriage contract for Chizuru makes perfect sense in on many planes. First, her father Yoshio seeks to elevate his importance in society. Let him think this arrangement will do just that. At the same time, Lord Mori will gain an ear into the politics of *Yedo*, and a mouthpiece also, should that ever become necessary. Second, the Mori *han* will extend its influence deep into Ryozuji territory, never a bad thing. And finally, a dowry of significance can never hurt the treasury reserves of the *han*. It does not occur to Lord Mori that Takazawa Yoshio may not have the ability to pay, but he does pause to wonder where such a handsome sum is coming from. A messenger is sent.

It is not possible to send a marriage arrangement proposal directly to Takazawa Yoshio. He is not of the Mori *han* nor does he abode in the Mori Domain. Instead, Lord Mori sends his escorted messenger to Lord Chiba of the Ryozuji *han* with a suitably expense gift, if not a recycled one from Takachika's aborted adventure to *Yedo*. It is a good thing that young Takachika had the sense to save the gift!

The messenger arrives at Lord Chiba's manor. He thanks Lord Chiba for his warm hospitality and on behalf of Lord Mori, he professes the unbreakable bond and everlasting friendship between the Mori and Chiba *han*. The gift is presented as is a sealed message requesting that Lord Chiba summon Takazawa Yoshio and present a marriage arrangement proposal to Takazawa Yoshio on behalf of Lord Mori. All proprieties observed.

Lord Mori's messenger and escort are afforded basic hospitality as their positions warrant. They wait while Lord Chiba considers.

In his private chambers, Lord Chiba debates the proposal with himself and out loud. "To allow Takazawa influence, however slight, into the Mori *han* only serves to weaken the house of Ryozuji. However, Takazawa's family and possessions are clearly here within my grasp should he need to be reminded where his loyalty lies. As a paid dog of the filth in *Yedo*, it might be good to divert their attentions away from the house of Ryozuji and to that of Mori instead. I can always leverage Takazawa's recent disregard of the Shogun's Separation Edict should I ever need to persuade him on one issue or another. Lastly, it is best to be on good terms with Mori. Unexplainable things seem to happen to those who cross him. Clearly, in my best interests to not only forward Lord Mori's proposal but to endorse it!"

Soon thereafter Lord Mori's messenger and escort are themselves escorted to *Shikimi* and to the residence of Takazawa Yoshio bearing the marriage arrangement proposal and a smaller token of sincerity.

"Takazawa Yoshio, our liege Lord, Mori Narimoto, Prince of *Nagato* and Lord of the *Choshu* Domain sends greetings. He proposes an arrangement of marriage between your legitimate daughter, Chizuru, and eldest son Takachika. The marriage could take place at *Hagi* Castle on an auspicious date of his choosing. The marriage would not be consummated, and bride and groom would live in segregated residence at *Hagi* Castle until the bride comes of age. This gift is offered as a token of my lord's sincerity. We will await your answer," declares the messenger in an official manner. He waits.

Yoshio cannot believe the good josh which has befallen him. The most powerful and wealthy *daimyo* in the region has made a marriage proposal for his Chizuru. Later he will thank his gods, but today he tries to compose himself and his answer. He does not even think to consult Chizuru.

Takazawa Yoshio bows deeply before the respective representatives of Lords Mori and Chiba. He strains to mask both anxiety and jubilation. He replies, "With the permission of Lord Chiba, the Takazawa family humbly accepts the unexpected marriage proposal of Lord Mori of the *Choshu* Domain. We thank him for the generous gift and look forward to whatever arrangements are made on Chizuru's behalf. May the gods bless houses of Mori and Ryozuji and long live the Son of Heaven."

It is done. The preparations begin.

Chizuru betrays little emotion when informed of her impending marriage to young Mori Takachika. She has never heard of him nor seen any likeness. She does not know what kind of boy he is or man he will become. She can only accept her fate. With the voice of the *kami* still resonating within her, she will follow the harsh path of this life without complaint. She visits the family shrine, and prays to the gods of her ancestors, the gods of *Shikimi*, then she prays to the God of the Cross, the One who revealed itself to her and will never forsake her. "Amen."

Chizuru's personal preparations are limited to packing her few possessions, treating her skin and hair, and hours in prayer and meditation. Her face and motions must reflect of a state of peace and beauty.

Yoshio communicates the marriage coup to his handlers. They are pleased of course, and have already forwarded the dowry gold to *Nagasaki* using their, as yet, undiscovered usual means of conveyance. Mori already suspects the dowry to be Tokugawan gold, but then Tokugawan gold is still gold and Takazawa can be manipulated in many ways. All seem to be satisfied with the arrangement.

Some months later, finally, the bridal party begins their journey north out of the Ryozuji Domain and into the southern-most territory controlled by the Mori *han*. The first half of the journey traverses the western and northwestern corner of modern *Kyushu* and terminates in the fishing village of *Togawa* on the *Seito Naikai*, the great Inland Sea of Japan. At *Togawa*, a vessel bearing the flag and *mon*, crest, of Lord Mori awaits the bridal party. From here they will make the short sea crossing to a sister village on the opposite side, *Shimonoseki*.

Upon arrival in *Shimonoseki*, Yoshio and the bridal party are greeted, refreshed and prepared for the continuation of their journey north. They are shocked when observing the heights surrounding the village of *Shimonoseki*. The heights are honey-combed with trenches and shelters and bristle with wheeled-canon on wooden platforms. Lord Mori's men are all about. The party passes through a veritable armed-camp as they make their way north toward *Hagi* Castle.

"We are at peace, why all the preparations for war," ponders Yoshio as they move up trail through the narrow pass from the beach to the high ground above the *Shimonoseki Straits*. Here the main road begins, taking a more or less direct route to *Hagi* Castle many *ri* to the north. They pass in silence.

The gates of *Hagi* Castle are open. The black and white *mon* of the Mori *han* decorate the walls and gates. All those living in and around the castle crowd around in an orderly sort of way, hoping to glimpse the bride to be. The *daijin* stand and stare, retainers, foot soldiers, peasants and servants nod their heads, bow slightly or deeply as the retinue approaches then passes. Lord Mori Narimoto and his son, Takachika await the bridal party, seated on an adorned dais in front of the great hall. The bridal stops before the dais. They all bow deeply. Chizuru has arrived at her new home.

Chapter Eleven
The Susquehanna

As official guests of the United States Government and observers aboard the *USS Susquehanna*, Jiro, Takeshi and Okada set sail with Commodore Perry and his squadron on April 1, 1854. Only the day before, a reluctant ruling counsel, on behalf of the Shogun Tokugawa Iesada, signed the Convention of Kanagawa which, in effect, rescinds the centuries-old policy of *sakoku*. Treaty in hand, the small squadron heads home via the China coast, Indian Ocean, Cape of Good Hope and ultimately Philadelphia. Navigating a circuitous route, promoting freedom of the seas, the showing of the flag and making ports of call, the transit to Philadelphia will take about one year.

The "guests" are allocated Midshipmen quarters. Cramped, spartan by any measure, their billet is considerably better than those of the common seamen and, though different, as good as any in his lordship's stable or even at the *Yushima Seido*. Shipboard fare, however, is only the first of their many culture shocks. Not yet familiar with shipboard routine, and not yet understanding a word of the American *gaijin* tongue, the trio is served their meal in quarters. Beef stew, hard tack, cheese, bread and butter, none of which they have ever seen or eaten before and all of it as unappetizing as the next. The Commodore, trying to provide his guests with some measure of comfort, sends his steward with a pot of china tea and several Mandarin oranges.

The young Negro steward points to the pot of stew set in front of them. Slowly and loudly he says, "Stew. This is stew. Stew." Okada smiles and bows. "*Obrigado*, thank you." The steward, with shiny white teeth accentuated by his coal-black skin, smiles and leaves the trio to their meal.

"I didn't know that there were black-skinned *gaijin*. Are they different than the white ones?" questions Takeshi.

Ignoring Takeshi's comment, Jiro complains, "Thank the gods for these *mikan*, Mandarin oranges, and tea! How can we survive with such shit for food? I can't stand the nauseating smell of it, let alone the taste. This food is every bit as foul as these filthy *gaijin* themselves."

"Do not allow the *gaijin* to sense, in anyway, your emotions. You must always avert your eyes, bow your heads and smile pleasantly. Say, *obrigado* for everything. *Sim*, yes, respond positively. These words are not the words of the American *gaijin* but of the *lingua portuguesa*. Perhaps, if, one of the crew understands these words, then we can begin to learn the American *gaijin* tongue also," instructs Okada. "I learned *Portugues* from the *Dejima* Island traders in *Nagasaki*. The essence of our mission is to learn but do not divulge, question, but do not answer, try all things, but do not demonstrate. In this way, you will retain an advantage," instructs Okada.

None of the trio have ever been aboard a ship before. The clockwork-like routine of the ship's company, all punctuated and ordered by the ship's bell fascinates them even if they are repulsed by these coarse, hairy, rank-smelling *gaijin* and their shit-like food. After a day or two however, hunger drives them to begin to pick at their meals. *Mikan* and tea are first to be consumed, later some bread and butter, eventually pieces of meat sorted-out of the salty brown gravy goo. Fortunate, too, is the initial course of the squadron. The squadron initially transits the calmer waters of the *Seito Naikai.* These first three days of smooth, shallow seas within sight of home islands do much to calm their anxieties and help them "get their sea legs." On the fourth day out, the squadron passes through the *Shimonoseki Straits* and into the Sea of Japan. This route, planned by the Commodore, will take them across the Tsushima Straits and directly to Busan on the Korean peninsula, their first port of call.

Busan is the most prominent trading port on the Korean peninsula. The Chinese, Dutch, Portuguese, English, Japanese and now the Americans have come to call.

Okada is excited to go ashore. Here the Japanese have maintained diplomatic and trading relations for hundreds of years. The Busan Waegwan is an important Japanese community. Here Okada can send a secret message back to *Yedo*, possibly find someone in the Japanese community with skills in the American tongue, and the trio can eat their first decent meal on over a week. Once ashore however, Okada takes his leave of the boys and goes to conduct his own business.

Left on their own, Jiro and Takeshi explore the streets, nooks and crannies close to the docks. Street vendors are in abundance here near the port. The boys find toasted rice balls, grilled squid with sweet soy sauce and Japanese-style pickles. Cross-cultural influences and geographic proximity make Korean-style food similar in many ways to that of Japan. These treats are consumed quickly with grunts and sighs of satisfaction replacing words. Finally, Jiro slows his eating and speaks. "By the gods this is delicious! We'll have to take some *onigiri* with us back aboard ship. Pickles too, they'll last a couple of weeks at least. I can't stand one more day of 'stew.' Hey, I just realized, I've actually learned an American *gaijin* word, 'stew.'"

"May the dogs of hell puke on it. I hate stew," responds Takeshi with a passion unusual for him. He takes another bite of squid off the skewer. "I wonder when Okada will return from the Busan Waegwan?"

"Back to what? Our bunks on the ship? To stew? He'll be drinking eating and drinking sake with the consulate until who knows when. Maybe he won't come back at all! We'll have to find our own entertainment. I think Okada mentioned *midoridori*, Green Street. I suspect we can find some teahouses there."

Takeshi, suddenly perks up. "Maybe the mama-san in Korea will be friendlier than those in *Yoshiwara*?"

"Don't count on it, Takeshi. These garlic-eating Koreans are *gaijin*, just as we are *gaijin* to them. They don't think of us as coming from 'The Land of Great Men.' Certainly, they'll accept our silver, even smile and bow, then they'll spit on our backs just as we turn to leave. We can pillow with them, but don't trust them. We are alone on this journey Takeshi. It's just you and me."

Green Street, just another dark, narrow alleyway not far from the port, is flanked by shabby "teahouses" quite unlike the walled, manicured-garden establishments in *Yoshiwara*. Like *Yoshiwara* they serve their clients a commodity in demand, but here without the discrimination, frills or cost. Without discernment, the boys enter the first establishment on the Street.

"*Hwongyong hamnida*, welcome, gentle sirs," greets a young Korean man near the front door. "How may we serve you? Tea, of course."

Jiro and Takeshi are led to the nearest table and seated as the young teahouse greeter calls toward the kitchen for tea. Korean-style tea and a snack of seasoned, dried squid is placed on the table before them by a shy-looking young girl. She pours each his tea, arranges the snack before them, and inquires, "*Hangulma hamnida ga*, do you speak Korean?" Quizzically the boys look at each other and shake their heads. After a moment, the young girl stands, bows and excuses herself in Korean. Before the boys can discuss this turn of events among themselves, the greeter is back questioning them.

"Is something wrong gentlemen? Was she not to your liking? Did she not serve you, or suit you? How may I help you further?" inquires the greeter.

Jiro responds, "We are not sure. No, she was very suitable. She said something in Korean, I think. We don't speak Korean. Then she left."

"Oh, I see. Yes, most of the ladies prefer to serve those who can speak our language. They are uncomfortable with those who cannot, even for pillowing. Let me see what I can do. You do have some silver, I presume?"

After a short while, the greeter returns from the back.

"Hyun-ok has agreed to entertain you gentlemen. You may pay me. Two pieces of silver each. If you are not satisfied with her entertainment, then come and see me. Please make yourselves comfortable," says the greeter. He then moves back to his station near the front door.

By the time Hyun-ok makes her appearance, the tea and snacks have been consumed and the boys are ready to proceed with their entertainment. Hyun-ok, by no surprise is not quite as young or fresh as the Korean server. She smiles, bows and greets them in Japanese. *"Konnichi wa, Noriko de gozaimasu,"* Good Day, I'm Hyun-ok but you may call me Noriko. Please follow me.

She leads them up a staircase in the back to her room, a surprisingly nice room. She lives here. In her broken Japanese, she asks who will be first. The second will have to wait on the chair outside her room until the first is finished. Takeshi wins and almost trips over himself to get inside the room and close the door before Jiro can object to the procedure or the win. Jiro sits down and waits.

Noriko beckons Takeshi to her bed, a real Western-type bed. Takeshi has never seen a bed before. Noriko sits on the side of the bed, and with Takeshi standing before her, she unbuttons his ship's trousers, revealing his *fundoshi*, Japanese-style loincloth, underneath. The anticipation and the unbuttoning of his trousers has brought Takeshi to a full erection. Continuing, she unties his *fundoshi* and pulls him on top of her. Gently taking him in her hand, she guides him into her waiting vagina. He ejaculates inside of her. In spite of the fact that he has already spent himself, he continues to hump her like a dog in heat. It is only when she rolls out from underneath him, he realizes that it is over. With some meekness, he says, *"Arigato*, thank you." Takeshi quickly dresses and ushers himself out of the room.

"Your turn, Jiro." Says Takeshi quickly and without looking at his friend.

"All right, fine. But how was it? What should I do?" asks Jiro almost in a panic.

"Just go in and stand in front of her. She'll take care of the rest, Jiro."

Jiro enters and says, *"Konnichi wa."* Noriko takes over from there.

On the way back to the Susquehanna, the boys, four silver *isshuban* lighter, cautiously at first, then in a more direct manner, discuss their "entertainments."

"I don't get it. What's so great about that? It was like sticking my *chinchin*, coll. penis, into a bowl of soup. I much preferred her hand," complains Takeshi.

"I have hands. Who needs it," adds Jiro.

The boys return to their berths below and amidships the *USS Susquehanna*, no longer virgins.

Two days later Okada also returns from Busan Waegwan. Trying to maintain the advantage, Okada says little, but questions much. He infers the boys have become men, if only by their unusual silence. The ship having taken on fresh supplies of water, victuals and coal prepares to leave port for the south China coast. The ship will transit the East Sea, the East China Sea and the Formosa Straits before making its next port of call at the international port of Hong Kong, some two weeks sail.

The first days passage are pleasant enough. The boys, unlike Okada, volunteer to help the men holystone the deck. It's hard work, but gives them something to do and ingratiates them just a little with the crew. While on their knees scrubbing the deck, they carefully watch how the crew conducts its business by task and by watch section. They study ropes, knots, sails, block and tackle. They try to understand.

After just a week at sea, and upon entering the Formosa Straits, the weather becomes foul. Low clouds and reduced visibility separate the ships of the squadron. Although a paddle-wheeler, the *Susquehanna* still uses sails to economize the use of coal and to improve speed. Strong winds buffet the sails, and the Commodore is obliged to secure the sails and continue at a slower speed under steam power. The *Susquehanna* wallows in the troughs of the foaming, greenish-white waves. Wind, clouds and showers drive all but watch sections below deck, where the stench of unwashed men combined with the odors of a urine and bile sluice sloshing about, produce an odor so vile as to make all but the oldest salt seasick.

The trio try to stay in their cabin, but the shaking ship, and the awful smell drive them topside to fresh air. Then wind and rain drive them below deck again and the process is repeats itself hour after hour until they fall exhausted into their bunks and sleep.

Just as all believe that they can stand it no longer, the weather begins to break, sails are again hoisted and the international port of Hong Kong is but three days away.

"I've heard the men refer to the storm as a typhoon. I imagine it to be the type of storm we call *taifu*. In Japan, some still refer to it as the *kamikaze*, Divine Wind, the horrible storm that destroyed the invading fleets of Kublai Khan during the reign of Emperor Go-Uda," instructs Okada.

"Whatever you call it, it was frightful. The only good to come of it is that no stew was served. I'm growing used to bread and butter, even the cold beans are tolerable," adds Takeshi.

The international port of Hong Kong is a beautiful, deep water port on the southern coast of China. The sprawling village, too large to be a village but too disorganized to be a city, clings like algae to the shoreline. Opposite, on the western side of the bay is the Portuguese colony of Macau. Macau is more organized, but tightly controlled by Portuguese authorities, thereby already becoming a backwater port by comparison to free-wheeling Hong Kong.

Unlike Busan, Hong Kong does not possess the cultural ties and influences with Japan. The architecture, sounds and smells are distinctly different here, but the small street vendors, grog shops and "entertainments," the same.

In port Hong Kong, the routine is much the same as was the case in Busan. The crew scatter about, and the officers conduct official and "unofficial" business. Okada seeks out Japanese diplomatic interests and the boys are left on their own to explore another new world. Their first order of business, as always, is food. Here the numerous street vendors offer some familiar items but the flavors and preparation quite unlike those in Japan or Korea. Sharper spices and wok frying dominate the offerings. Jiro and Takeshi eat well nevertheless. With a limited supply of coin, and experience gained in both *Yoshiwara* and Green Street, the "entertainments" of Hong Kong appear somewhat less attractive than before. Still they wander, look and inquire. Here, inquiries soon uncover something new in their limited experience, opium. Like grog shops, bars and teahouses, opium dens are plentiful.

Though uninitiated and unwarned, the boys are wary of the dens and manage to resist their powerful draw. The same cannot be said for all the American crew however and trouble follows. Under the twin influences of liquor and opiates, two of the squadron's crew members succumb to their more base instincts, jealousy and greed. One Bosun's mate falls into argument after waking up from a drug-induced sleep and feeling disoriented. He beats the den-house owner senseless and bloody, then staggers back to the ship. Port authorities soon follow and protest the behavior. The mate is placed in confinement until his time before the mast. The other, a more serious offense, occurs when an ill-tempered carpenter's mate, unfortunately carrying with him some of the tools of his trade, knifes another foreign sailor in an "entertainment" dispute. The carpenter is returned to the ship in irons.

The Commodore, seemingly never happy, is pleased nonetheless to be a sea again. Hong Kong is a dirty, crowded hole with too many competing nations and motivations. It simply confuses the more simple and straight-forward man that he is. His flagship however carries with it left-over dirty business from the port of call which the Commodore's second in command must attend to. The two confinees are brought before the mast, heard and sentenced. The less serious offender is given a harsh but reasonable sentence by a clearly irritated presiding officer.

He reads out the accused. "By God you should be flogged! You can thank your lucky stars that the Congress these five years past have tied my hands. So, unable as I am to flog the tar out of you, I sentence you to confinement below, in irons, for a period of not less than thirty days. Your only sustenance shall be hardtack and water. Now get out of my sight!"

He is taken away.

The second confinee is brought before the Captain. "Carpenter's Mate Jackson, you have been found guilty of assault and attempted murder of a fellow seaman while under the influence of grog and opium. You have tarnished the name of this great ship, its crew and your flag. Your victim may still perish from his wounds. You will never know. Because you, Carpenter's Mate Jackson are sentenced to be hanged by the neck until dead, at noon on this day. May God have mercy on you, because I will have none!"

Before noon, the entire ship's company is assembled on deck to witness punishment, the Bosun's mate in his irons, the crew, officers and Japanese guests. The condemned is brought forward. While he is being bound arms and legs, he spits and yells, "A pox on you all." He is hooded and hauled up the yardarm where he hangs until he is dead.

The Captain whispers to another officer standing by his side, "Nothing is more foul than an unrepentant man. Surely he will burn."

The hanged, swinging from his rope, twitches and jerks for a period of time. Jiro and Takeshi among others who have never witnessed capital punishment, are mesmerized in a negative way.

"There is no honor is such a death," whispers Takeshi.

"A foul death for a foul man," quips Jiro.

After a time, the hanged is brought down, the crew returns to stations, and the squadron steams on.

Energies and money spent in ports of call, a mate in irons, another hanged, all serve to temper the crew. With some exceptions, they turn to their vocation as distraction enough for the remainder of the voyage home. Okada makes observations as Jiro and Takeshi try to integrate and learn from the habits and language of the men and routine of the ship. Philadelphia is still dozens of servings of stew away, as they look forward to even bigger events and discoveries in the United States of America.

Chapter Twelve
On the Bay

*I*n the late spring, after the fields and gardens have been tilled and planted, David has time to uncover "Ketch of the Day" and begin to fit her out. Since winterizing her last fall, David has worked hard at the Leonardstown *Democrat Observer* to repay Mr. MacDonald's advances on wages, his father's loan and to save some money towards the refitting. David has done well at the newspaper, learning and moving quickly with his assigned tasks. One day, after hearing numerous complaints about wandering livestock in and around Leonardstown, he convinces his boss, the owner and editor, to let him write a commentary about the matter. Young David is in print for the first time.

```
Nuisance Cows

My dear readers,
```

We consider it common sense and consensus, that wandering livestock does not belong in town. This newspaper has received numerous complaints about animals without owners promenading the streets and alleyways, eating gardens and making deposits in inconvenient places. These beasts are being cursed on a regular basis.

It is the opinion of this newspaper however, that it is not the wandering livestock that is to blame. We contend that it is owner neglect and the poor state of fences in this township that is well-source of these delinquencies. Let us then blame the negligent owners and possibly fine them two bits for each errant beast. The proceeds can be used for sidewalk improvements and we contend that the cases of nuisance cows will greatly diminish.

"David, what a nice editorial. My livestock-owning subscribers will be angry for sure. No doubt some may even threaten to cancel their subscriptions, but we'll go with it. Good job!" compliments Mr. MacDonald.

"Thank you, sir. I'm glad you like it. I just said it like it is."

During the late fall, winter and early spring months, David's book connection with the library in Annapolis has paid him handsome informational dividends. He has received and studied many recent books and manuals on refitting, sailing and navigation. David is preparing himself for a summer on the bay. Still much work remains to be done. When classes finally recess for the summer, his renewed work on "Ketch of the Day" begins.

The masts and booms are reasonably solid. The sheets and lines are either gone or unserviceable. Henry has used his connections to find David some well-used sheets that can be fabricated in mainsails and jibs, used line is readily available. The work is tedious, monotonous, but rewarding in the end. All summer David toils, always with advice and often with a helping hand from Henry. By August's end, the "Ketch of the Day" is repaired, refitted and ready to go.

On the appointed day, David, Henry and Nathan, with block and lever, ease the boat back toward the high tide line. David has consulted the almanac in order to determine the highest tide, therefore the least work in refloating his pride. With great effort, they manage to push her back to a point where the high tide should refloat her, then they wait. As the afternoon tide slowly rises, David wonders if they have pushed her far enough toward the water's edge. But the tide continues to rise and so does David's hopes. Finally, at high tide, there is enough water beneath the boat, lifting her enough, that the three are able push her fully into the bay.

"Hurrah, hurrah for us. We did it! The 'Ketch of the Day' is seaworthy again," hollers David.

"Not so fast, son. Refloated yes, but seaworthy is not a word we'll use until we've taken 'er out on a 'shakedown' cruise. We'll anchor 'er here for the night. If she's still afloat on the morrow, then we'll see if our work for these past two summers is worth the sweat we've spent," cautions Henry.

"Oh yes, please, let's give her some time to settle back into the water. I've never been on a boat before. I shouldn't like to sink," interjects Nathan.

"I can agree to that. Tonight she lies at anchor. Tomorrow we sail!" agrees David

On the next morning, after chores, the crew of "Ketch of the Day" gathers at the beach and is collectively relieved to see the proud little boat resting at anchor on the bay.

"She looks good. Not low in the water at all. Let's go aboard and give 'er a run up the bay," exclaims David.

Henry spits some chew on the beach, Irish coffee in hand, and nods.

The three wade out to the ketch and climb aboard.

"We need to get a dingy. I'm soaked before we start," complains Nathan.

"Let's hope we don't get wetter by day's end," adds Henry as he takes another swig of his fortified brew.

As "captain" of his vessel, David orders the anchor be raised and the "Ketch of the Day" drifts out away from shore. The aft mainsheet is unfurled, and secured, then the jib. A small wake forms astern of the boat, the "Ketch of the Day" is finally and truly underway.

David, as "captain" and helmsman, mans the rudder, Henry manages the sheets and rigging, Nathan stand by, somewhat in awe, assisting Henry when told to do so. Henry has wisely decides to keep the forward mainsheet furled so that the undermanned and landlubber crew might manage to stay ahead of the boat. With a slight breeze coming up the bay from the southeast, David tacks the boat slightly to starboard, then turning the bow west by northwest out of the bay and into the Potomac Sound. The breeze freshens as they move away from the influence of the shore and out into the western Chesapeake.

Without experience or charts there is always a danger of inadvertently finding a mud flat and running aground. The previous owner of the ketch, may, perhaps attest to this. Henry, an experienced man, watches out for any change in the color of the waters or pattern of the waves. Clouds passing overhead influence the waters color, potentially deceiving the sailors, but the ever-changing Sound is relatively deep here, and no other hazards to navigation are encountered.

For an hour or more they let 'er run with the wind. Some bilge water sloshes in the bottom, but she seems to be tightly sealed, a testament to the original shipwright as well as the time and patience David and Henry have devoted to the hull. At 1200 hours, it is time to make for home, Breton Bay and Leonardstown. David jibs hard to the port, the booms pivot on their axis and the sheets go slack. She's turned into the wind but is not yet tacking properly. The Potomac current and tide carries them eastward toward the sea. The wind-whipped waves move westward up the Sound. An unusual phenomena for sure, but in control or not, they slowly drift back toward Breton Bay and Leonardstown.

David finds that the theory of tacking against the wind is somewhat different than handling a boat and tacking in practice.

Henry leaves his post at the sheets and riggings to Nathan and assists the new helmsman.

"It's really a bit of an art rather than a science, Davie. Hold the rudder, look out across the waves, then up at the sheets. Calculate in your head the direction and velocity of the wind. Tack at just enough of an angle to fill the sheets, secure your lines and work that direction until you need to change in order to stay on your general course. Tacking is just another way of saying zigzag the way to your destination," instructs Henry.

Davie, already understanding the concept, begins to learn the practice. They tack southeast, then east-northeast and back again until they gradually make their way around Colton's Point and back into Breton Bay. The little ketch has proved herself seaworthy again, as have the novice, skeleton-crew of two boys and an old man. They have successfully worked her out and up the Sound and back home again.

Thereafter, every week for the rest of the summer and late into the fall, David, Henry and Nathan run the "Ketch of the Day" out of Breton Bay into the Sound. They sail up the western shore of Maryland and back down the eastern shore of Virginia. David has acquired a used chart and uses this as a basis of his navigation, making copious notes thereupon and demonstrating to Henry an acumen and a passion for what will ultimately become his vocation. For the next two summers, David continues his work at the Leonardstown *Democrat Observer* and sails "Ketch of the Day" at every opportunity. With his father's blessing, he writes a letter to the Honorable Samuel Smith, United States Senator for Maryland, seeking appointment as a Midshipman in the fledgling United States Navy. His letter is endorsed by his father, Miss

Madson, Mr. MacDonald and the County Sheriff. His hopes now lie with Senator Smith in Washington, D.C.

The Honorable Samuel Smith
United States Senate

Dear Senator Smith,

I, David S. McDougal of Leonardstown, Maryland seek the assistance of your office in securing a position as a Midshipmen in the Navy of our country.

I have graduated from the Leonardstown Normal School and worked these past three years as an apprentice at the Leonardstown Democrat Observer.

Although commonly educated, I am very literate, an industrious worker and God-fearing constituent of our State of Maryland. I am self-taught and experienced in boat-building, sailing and nautical navigation.

Prominent citizens of Leonardstown have endorsed my appeal in regards to this matter.

Accordingly, I request your serious consideration of my appeal and thank you most sincerely for any help or advice you may be able to offer.

Your servant,

On April 1, 1828, David is appointed as a Midshipman initially aboard the *USS Congress* at nearby Norfolk, Virginia. David's life-long vocation has begun.

Chapter Thirteen
Keikonshiki (The Wedding)

The arrival of the wedding party from *Shikimi* is an event of great interest and some importance to all at *Hagi* Castle, that is, except the intended bridegroom Takachika. Takachika, still brooding from his near death experience on the *Tokaido* Road, takes no interest in his prospective bride or the planned event. Young Takachika paces around an upper floor of the castle looking down on the entourage in the courtyard below, talking to himself.

"She is not a foreign princess. She is not of noble blood. She is not even exceptionally pretty. One slit is the same as the next. Why her? She's not of age, I'm not of age, why a wedding now when father should be dealing with the dogs in *Yedo* who ordered me killed."

Takachika is working himself into an emotional froth, when the door slides open and Counselor Takahashi enters.

"Young lord, your presence is expected on the dais. Your father is asking for you. The wedding party has arrived and you must greet them."

"I have no interest in greeting fishmongers from *Shikimi!*" contemptuously replies Takachika.

"Interest or no interest, your father has summoned you. I strongly suggest that you do not cross your father. Go, smile pleasantly, and receive our guests. It is your duty to the *han.*"

"Always duty to the *han.* Whenever you have no other valid argument, it is always, 'your duty to the *han.*' You need a new entreaty, Takahashi! All right, I will go."

In the outdoor courtyard, upon his dais, Lord Mori Narimoto sits quietly considering the arriving entourage before him. The father of the bride, Takazawa Yoshio, is unimpressive. He wears a *kamishimo*, vest, imprinted with the *mon* of the Tokukawa, a symbol of his office, officially, Customs Officer of *Shikimi*. Lord Mori does not need to be reminded that he is opening the gates of *Hagi* Castle to a dog of *Yedo*. Takazawa's wife, Eko, is absent; it is of no consequence. Gift bearers, servants and retainers of the Ryozuji *han*, and, of course, the intended bride make up the balance of the entourage. Lord Mori looks down at the bride to be, Chizuru. He looks her up and down in a lustful and unfatherly manner and talks to himself. "Not really a comely girl, she seems a bit too fragile for childbearing, but acceptable for play. I'll bang her once myself before the wedding and make certain that she is a virgin, at least until I get done with her. Takachika's too inexperienced to know the difference."

Takachika arrives on the dais. His arrival is acknowledged by Lord Mori. Young Takachika grudgingly concludes the formalities required of him. All bow, the first meeting of the two families is over. Servants lead the family of the bride to their quarters, a comfortable and respectable suite made ready for their extended stay. After a voluminous evening meal is served and consumed in their quarters, Takazawa Yoshio dons a *yukata*, light robe of cotton or silk, and retires to the bath. The lord's bath at *Hagi* Castle is a natural hot springs and consists of two areas; the first a quaint, Cedar-board building for changing, bathing and sitting. The second area, only a few stones step distant, is an open-air bath for enjoyment in fair weather. Yoshio steps into the open-air bath, small towel soaked in cold water atop his head, and sits down on a large, flat-top stone placed just below the surface. The hot water and rising steam engulf his body. He sighs, and relaxes for the first time today.

Within minutes another guest arrives at the bath. Yoshio has seen the withered, older gentleman before, yes, next to Lord Mori on the dais. Takahashi speaks first.

"Takazawa-*sama*, honorific – my good gentleman Takazawa, I am Takahashi, Counselor to Lord Mori Narimoto, as I was Counselor to his father before him. I chose this place to speak with you, because we are somewhat beyond suspicion here in the bath and this place has no walls. In all the years of my service, I have seen and heard many things. Sometimes it would be good for others, outside the *Choshu* Domain to hear these things. Consider my words, and we shall speak again."

"Yes, Counselor Takahashi. I will consider your words most seriously and in the greatest confidence."

"This is good. Because truly I say to you, if even the slightest suspicion develops that we have shared these words, we will both surely die before the sun sets that day."

Counselor Takahashi wades to the opposite side of the open-air bath, now he sighs and relaxes for the first time in many years.

Days come and go at *Hagi* Castle. The Takazawa entourage fall into a new routine: wait, eat, shuffle around, and wait again. Lord Mori presides over business as usual, paying little attention to the preparations being made on behalf of his illegitimate son and heir, Takachika or to his guests in the east suite of the castle. Yoshio dislikes his new routine, a routine where he is not the master, but the pawn of the master. He can't wait to marry off Chizuru, leave *Hagi* Castle and return to *Shikimi.* Yoshio and Counselor Takahashi have several more brief encounters prior to the wedding. They greet one another, mumble a few polite words and pass. In one such exchange however, their eyes meet and Yoshio nods in agreement. It is settled. The conduit to *Yedo* is established.

"Come here, girl. You have no need to fear your lord and father-in-law to be. I wish to speak with you," commands Lord Mori.

"Yes, my lord."

"Slide the door shut and come stand in front of me. Look at me. How old are you?"

"I am fifteen, I believe, my lord."

"Fifteen. Have you become a woman?"

"Yes, my lord. Two summers ago."

"*Naruhodo,* I see. Have you ever known a man? A boy?"

"No, my lord."

"Not a man? Not a boy? Not another girl, I trust?"

Chizuru does not answer. She is becoming frightened. These questions are unseemly, improper. Yes, she should be frightened. He is as evil as his son will someday be.

"Pull up your kimono, and bend over, there against the wall. I'm going inspect you and make certain that you're not just some fishmonger's slut."

"Please my lord, do not violate me. I beg of you!" pleads Chizuru.

Tears welling up in her eyes, she follows Lord Mori's command. Hands above her head, bracing against the nearest wall, she hikes up her kimono and bends over. As she does so, in an inaudible whisper she prays to the God of the Cross. "Oh my God, intercede on my behalf. Protect my womb from violation. Protect my person from harm. You saved me once from death by disease, save me now from death by shame. You are my *kami*, you are always with me, I am always with you. I pray thee. Amen."

Lord Mori removes his *hakama*, traditional trousers worn over a men's kimono, wearing only his *fundoshi* from the waist down, he examines her. He pays no attention to her protests or her whispers. He slowly caresses her flawless white buttocks so small and firm. He expects her breasts to be the same but wrapped tightly in her multi-layered kimono, they are too difficult to grab. Uncharacteristically, he fumbles with the ties on his *fundoshi*. Typically he is excited by instilling fear. Today however, he is unmoved. He fondles her again, more roughly this time. He tries to stimulate himself. Still, nothing. He is as limp as a jellyfish on the beach. Angrily, he dismisses her even before he has pulled his *hakama* back up to his waist.

"You'll do. Get out!" he commands.

"Thank you, my lord, thank you."

Chizuru straightens her kimono and hurries to escape from the room, forgetting protocol and forgetting to shut the door.

The day of the wedding at hand, all gather at the Mori family shrine for the ceremony. The bride, Chizuru is dressed in a magnificent wedding kimono adorned with symbols of prosperity and longevity. The white silk headdress worn by all brides, is said to hide horns beneath. In ancient times, weddings were performed at night, but now, particularly in the cases of *daimyo* weddings, the Shogunate allows the ceremony to take place during the day.

Quite contrary to his social station, Takazawa Yoshio pays a significant dowry in gold to the Mori *han*. The handsome dowry, although welcomed, is a matter of consternation to Lord Mori, in that he again ponders the actual source of the money. Young Takachika performs his duty to the *han* as instructed by Counselor Takahashi and demanded by Lord Mori.

"This fishmonger's daughter from *Shikimi* is of no consequence," reasons Takachika. "When I become lord of the *Choshu* Domain, I will just lock her away and do what I will with whomever I desire. The girl will not inconvenience me in the slightest."

Young Takachika goes through the motions of the ceremony, never looking at or speaking to his bride. When the banquet is held in the new couple's honor, he drinks, eats, speaks a few words with his father, Counselor Takahashi and a few of the *daijin*, headmen of the *han*. When the wedding banquet is concluded, the under-age bride returns with her family to their suite. Young Takachika returns to his quarters and routine as though he was not married.

Counselor Takahashi now has his conduit, the *bakufu* now have their spy and young Takachika awaits the day when he will become lord of the *Choshu* Domain.

Chapter Fourteen
And Justice for All

"Well, good morning, Mr. Pruyn. We are so pleased to have you, a university man, join our humble firm," greets Mr. Erasumus Vanderhornt.

"Good morning to you, sir. It is truly an honor to join you here at Vanderhornt, Klatt, and Becht. I really never imagined apprenticing to such a prestigious firm, and right here in my hometown of Albany," responds Robert enthusiastically.

"Well, it is good that you are here. Your father has been soliciting on your behalf these past three years. It will be interesting to finally see if you are as bright and hardworking as he says you are."

"Thank you, sir. I will thank father later."

"Now, down to business. I have a case for you."

"A case, sir? I have not yet started my apprenticeship."

"Ah, It'll be good for you. A few depositions, a little research, draw on your debating skills perhaps and *voila*, there you go, a trial lawyer. Besides, it is not a capital case, so no one is going to

die if you lose. Further, it is *pro bono* for an immigrant family, so it is also unlikely that the firm will be accused of predatory practices or of over-charging the client."

"I am still concerned, sir, but if you think."

"Yes, I think. And besides again, they are right off the boat from Dublin, so you know they're guilty of something. But the mother has been bleating around town about her innocent boys. Making a lot of noise she is. So, therein lies our opportunity! No worries, I'll be looking over your shoulder. Just make a good show of it!" orders Mr. Vanderhornt with finality.

"Yes, sir. I'll try to make a good show of it," answers Robert. "What are the particulars of the case?"

"I don't know much more than I've read here in the newspaper. The constable contacted me once he had made the arrests and asked if I had any ideas about their defense. I offered our services out of hand. I thought that it might make good press and all, Vanderhornt and Co defending penniless immigrants. Now, you go make it happen."

"Yes, sir. I will try to not disappoint you, sir."

"Oh, don't worry about disappointing me Robert. Worry about disappointing our clients. And while you're at it, generate some press!"

Mr. Vanderhornt hands Robert a copy of the Albany Evening Journal. Robert sits down at "his" desk and begins to read.

```
Citizen Assaulted
In the early evening hours of
Wednesday, Mr. W.H. Acuff of 56 W
Chester Street in this fair city was
```

assaulted by a knife-wielding suspect. The assailant demanded Mr.
Acuff's money, of which he is said
to have carried thirty-five dollars
and fifty cents in mixed gold and
silver specie. Additionally, the
goon relieved Mr. Acuff of his gold
watch, chain, pearl tie pin and gold
cuff links. The total value of
stolen property being greater than
$75. Although Mr. Acuff did not
clearly see his assailant, two sus-
picious persons, foreign transients, were later arrested trying
to sell Mr. Acuff's tie pin to the
town jeweler. They are currently re-
siding in the city jail awaiting
trial. This newspaper compliments
Constable Owens on the timely arrests and looks forward to a speedy
trial and just sentencing by Judge
Henry Wadsworth.

Robert sits for a moment longer, then with newspaper in hand
walks down to the city jail to introduce himself to his first clients.

"So, you found the pin?" repeats Robert incredulously.

"Yes sir, we found it near our camp site by the river. We came
by steamer to Albany and were going to continue west on the Erie
Canal. We haven't a lot of money and we, that is my brother and

I, were real excited when we found the pin. We figured it was gold and pearl and that we could sell it for a few dollars, which we did. The constable arrested us shortly thereafter as we were returning to our campsite," states Marley, one of the brothers.

"I see. I'll ask the constable to release you to my custody and we'll I'll wander out and take a look see at the site of your discovery."

Constable Owen "releases" suspect Marley to Robert's custody, accompanied by his deputy. They take a short walk down a well-worn and muddy path leading to the riverside campsite of the immigrants. Marley points out the site of discovery.

"Here you say. So close to your campsite? Did you hear or see anyone?" queries Robert.

"No, sir."

"There are footprints here in the mud. Let's see if we can find a clear one. Ah, yes, here. It's rather large. We'll measure it with my watch chain. Take note, there's a diagonal mark on the print. The mark could be a flaw or damage to the sole of the shoe or boot and could help us identify the specific owner," notes Robert. "That's all from here, I think. Deputy, we can return now."

A week later the immigrant boys, two good-looking lads in their late teens, are brought to trial before Judge Henry Wadsworth. Many of the townspeople crowd the courtroom, predisposed in their thoughts regarding the guilt or innocence of these transient immigrants.

"All rise. The Honorable Henry Wadsworth presiding," barks the bailiff.

The city prosecutor begins, "The defendants in this case are not of our fine city. They are outsiders to our city, our citizens and to our laws. Our city, all of us, have suffered a dreadful crime, a violent crime. We fear for our persons as we walk down our streets. This is because, one of us, a law-abiding citizen, Mr. W.H. Acuff, sitting right over there, was walking home from his office, minding his own business, when he was accosted at knife point by these two outlaw and foreign boys. They threatened his body with harm and took from his money, watch, cuff links and tie pin. We know this because they were foolish enough to try to sell part of their ill-gotten booty to Mr. Silbermann, our town jeweler. Mr. Acuff's money, watch and cuff links have not been recovered, but the gold and pearl tie pin are Exhibit Number One here before the court. In that neither brother have demonstrated any contrition, nor a willingness to confess or testify against the other, the City of Albany asks you, men of the jury to look at this evidence and pass judgment on their guilt."

"Now, Mr. Prosecutor," begins Robert. "Too much! My clients are innocent of these charges. These boys were neither seen by Mr. Acuff, nor did they have in their possession any of Mr. Acuff's valuables, save his tie pin which they found on the trail near their campsite. These are poor travelers. Goods and services are expensive, so naturally they offered to sell their fortunate find to Mr. Silbermann for a few extra dollars. Any of us would have done the same."

"Call your first witness, Mr. Prosecutor," states the judge flatly.

"Mr. Acuff please come forward, take the oath and be seated here on the witness stand. Now Mr. Acuff, will you share with the court, your experience of Wednesday two weeks past."

Mr. Acuff recalls closing shop, walking toward home and the assault. He confirms the details as written in the constable's report and the newspaper.

Robert cross-examines, "Mr. Acuff, did you see your assailant(s)?"

"No, sir. I did not see **them**."

"If you did not see **them**, then how do you know there were more than one? Did you hear more than one?"

"I guess I don't know that, sir."

"Did you see the weapon, the knife?"

"No, sir. I did not actually see the knife, but I **felt** it."

"**Felt** it? Did it cut you?

"No, sir. It did not cut me. I was wearing a greatcoat. But, I felt it for sure."

"I see. You neither saw the perpetrator nor the knife, yet you use the plural 'assailants' and the adjective 'knife-wielding.' Could it not been a finger or a stick that poked you in the back? Could it not have been some person other than these traveling pilgrims that assaulted you?"

"Yes, sir. I suppose that is a possibility."

"That is all, Your Honor." Robert turns to sit down. In turning to sit and with the light coming through the window, he notices a slight reflection off the wrist of a spectator. Curious, Robert maneuvers in his chair to observe the spectator more closely. He knows of this man, a local boy named Lawrence Bracht.

Robert has an idea. He asks for a short recess. He confers with Constable Owen.

"Constable Owen, do you know Lawrence Bracht? Has he ever been in any trouble here in Albany?"

"Lawrence? Sure, I know him. Trouble, not really. He a local boy, works here and there at odd jobs. Not employed at the moment, I think. He can be a little loud, a little boisterous and little rough with some liquor in him. Not a big problem."

125

"Well, constable, I have a hunch. I have a hunch that Lawrence knows something more about this assault. Would you do me two favors: first, post a deputy at the back door, and second, just wander over and see if Lawrence is wearing cuff links."

"Cuff links? Are you joking? Why would a young man in overalls be wearing cuff links?"

"Like I said, just a hunch," replies Robert.

During the court-granted, short recess, Constable Owens leisurely walks by Lawrence Bracht mingling with the crowd. Lawrence becomes uncomfortable being in close proximity to the constable and slowly moves toward the door where he is suddenly stopped by a deputy.

"Now, you let me go. You have no right keeping me in here," he tells the deputy in an agitated manner.

"Constable says to hold you here. Here you stay!" says the deputy.

The constable follows Lawrence to the door and casually asks, "Lawrence, where did you get those cuff links?"

"Ugh, them fellas over there in irons sold 'em to me"

"Sold them to you? When?"

"Ugh, last Saturday at the market."

Constable Owen smiles a little, and Lawrence relaxes. "Oh, sure, last Saturday. They must have passed 'em through the jail-house window, I guess? Lawrence, why don't you come along with me and we'll sit up front here so that we can watch these fellas get what's coming to 'em."

"Nah, Owen. I best be getting on towards home. I've seen enough of this show. I know they'll get what coming to 'em."

"No, Lawrence. You stay with me here. Peaceful like or in cuffs, your choice."

"I'll always be peaceful when there's no other choice."

The trial recommences, and Robert calls a witness. Witness Lawrence Bracht of Albany.

"Lawrence, do you spend much time down by the river?"

"Some, sir. I fish when they're biting."

"You're a big man, Lawrence, you have big hands and feet?"

"Feet aren't the only thing I've got that big, sir."

The crowd laughs uproariously. Judge Wadsworth is not amused and gavels the court to order.

"How big would you say your shoes are Lawrence, bout as long as my watch chain?"

"Why do you ask?"

"Because Lawrence, I think you know who robbed Mr. Acuff on Wednesday two weeks past."

"Yeah, it was them fellas. They had his tie pin!"

"And you, Lawrence, you have his cuff links! You know the ones you bought from um when they were in the city jail. Did you also buy a gold watch and chain with the thirty-seven dollars?"

Robert turns toward the bench and declares. "I submit to this court that it is Lawrence Bracht, not my clients, who robbed Mr. Acuff at knife-point. I believe that he dropped the tie pin near the immigrant camp so to implicate the foreign travelers regardless of whether or not they would find the pin. I further submit, that if the court will examine the right shoe sole of Mr. Lawrence, it will find a diagonal gash, which being consistent with the footprint at the site of discovery, then places Mr. Lawrence at said site along the river. All of this corroborates the story of my clients and casts grave doubt on their guilt if not proves their innocence.

Accordingly, I move that the charges against my clients be dismissed and Mr. Lawrence be taken into custody!"

Judge Wadsworth nods his head in agreement. He frowns, then orders, "The charges against Messrs. Marley and Terrance O'Malley are dismissed without prejudice. This court orders them released immediately. Bailiff, take Mr. Bracht into custody. Court is adjourned!"

The crowd of locals let up a collective gasp at the turn of events. All eyes are focused on Lawrence Bracht as he is taken away. Mr. Vanderhornt rushes forward to congratulate Robert. Forgotten are the O'Malley brothers, who, only minutes ago were the focus of Albany's collective ire.

"Good show Robert! An impressive debut for our new 'apprentice.' You are destined to become someone."

Chapter Fifteen
Perseverance and Hope

The wedding is over. Takazawa Chizuru is now a member of the Mori *han*. Though a member, she feels isolated, a stranger. Takazawa Yoshio can't leave *Hagi* Castle quick enough. He packs his travel belongings and prepares to depart. He advises his now married daughter one last time.

"Chizuru, I have been away from *Shikimi* far too long. I must return to my official duties and to your mother. You are now a member of a powerful *han*. You must endeavor to persevere. But, if you ever have the need to communicate important matters beyond the confines of *Hagi* Castle or the *Choshu* Domain, trust Counselor Takahashi. He will help you, of this I am certain. Good bye, daughter."

Chizuru stands in the middle of the suite, shoulders slumped, hands at her side, tearing rolling down her cheeks. She is not particularly sad that her father is leaving, he never did pay her much mind, but she is fearful of the uncertainty of her future.

Each evening, before dark and before his evening meal, Lord Mori strolls down to the small Cedar-board bathhouse in his *yukata* to take his twice daily bath. He quickly disrobes, throws the *yukata* in a wicker basket and immerses himself in the hot springs satisfying waters. When he emerges refreshed, sometime later, he again dons the *yukata*, ties the *obi*, cloth belt, and returns alone to his private chambers. During his bath however, a poisonous Redback spider has crawled out from the dark, warm space beneath the Cedar floor boards and taken refuge in the folds of his garment. Hidden there, unseen, the spider bites his victim on his tender inner thigh. Lord Mori feels the prick, swats, then scratches and continues on without giving the matter much thought.

On the next morning Lord Mori awakens with a large red lump punctuated by a dark hole in the center on his inner thigh. He vaguely remembers the prick and gives the matter no further thought. By following day, the large red lump has become a painful, angry swelling extending from his groin to knee. He does not sleep well, is feverish and cold. When he walks or talks, he feels slightly disoriented.

By the third day, neither the pain nor the swelling have abated. His scrotum and left testicle are now part of the problem. An ugly red line extends from the center of the bite into his groin. In spite of his doctor's best efforts, the fever worsens and convulsions follow. On the fifth day, Lord Mori Narimoto lapses into a coma and dies before the sun sets that day.

The next day the announcement is made.

Lord Mori Narimoto, Prince of *Nagato*, Lord of the *Choshu* Domain has gracefully passed from the world of the living. He has entered the world of the spirits and his ancestors. The traditional forty-nine days of mourning shall be observed by all.

Officially celebrated and mourned, Lord Mori Narimoto is missed by no one. If only those at *Hagi* Castle, the *daijin* of the Domain, and the people knew the future under young Mori Takachika, some would gladly make a journey into the spirit world to bring Lord Mori Narimoto back.

At his wake, lying there in his white silk "death" kimono, Lord Mori Narimoto does not appear as frightening as he could be in life. Sitting beside him through the night, young Takachika begins to relax a little. He talks to himself. "Father is gone. In forty-nine days I become Lord Mori, Prince of *Nagato*, Lord of the *Choshu* Domain. After that, I will only have to deal with him during *obon*, ghost festival. Ha! Life is full of surprises, isn't it, father. But the biggest surprise of all was losing life and finding yourself in the world of the spirits. But do not fear for the sake of the *han*, I will prove to be its good steward. But, beware *bakufu*, you wished **me** on the funeral pyre, not him, but still I live. Beware all who conspire against me or the *han*, for you shall suffer horribly, and only die at my pleasure. Long live The Son of Heaven. Long live the *han*. And, long live **me**!"

Chizuru pays her due respects to her late father-in-law, following all proprieties, before retreating back to the shelter of her suite. Although surrounded by supportive and loyal handmaidens, she knows that she will be called for and somehow senses a dark and unhappy life as Lady Mori. She prays to her *kami* and resolves to propose divorce before being called and before the marriage can be consummated.

Chizuru meets with young Takachika in private and begs to be released from the marriage contract.

"My lord, I was summoned to *Hagi* Castle by agreement between your late father, Lord Mori Narimoto and my father. You did not choose me and I sense that I disappoint you. Please divorce me. Send me back. The shame is on me. I beg you."

For the first time Takachika considers the young girl kneeling before him. She is not displeasing to the eye; her body is slim and firm. He doesn't seriously consider her plea, rather is more concerned at the moment with the fact that he hasn't had a woman or girl during these past days of mourning. He disliked his father, but doesn't wish to anger the spirit world by violating taboos. He briefly considers fucking her then sending her away, but instead, uncharacteristically answers her directly and honestly.

"No, I cannot divorce you. I, myself, am the illegitimate son of our late lord Narimoto. It is true, I am the rightful heir, but not the son of his proper wife. He has chosen you for me. The Shogun has approved the marriage. Your father has paid a huge dowry in gold. We are married, and you provide legitimacy to me. You will bear my legitimate children, and I, in turn, will have heirs. No, after the mourning period is over, and I become the Lord Mori, you will come to me and we will be husband and wife. Whether you are happy or unhappy is of no consequence to me. You will be Lady Mori Takachika. It is for the good of the *han.* Accept the will of the gods!"

After forty-nine days of mourning, at the age of seventeen, young Mori Takachika becomes the thirteenth *daimyo* of the *Choshu* Domain. Takachika is now Lord Mori Takachika, Prince of *Nagato,*

Lord of the *Choshu*. Chizuru, his wife, against her wishes and all probability is now Lady Mori Takachika. While Chizuru endeavors to persevere, trusts in her *kami*, and places hope in a faith she little understands, Lord Mori now takes reign of the *Choshu* Domain. He rules with an iron hand beholden only to his Emperor, the Son of Heaven. He becomes the antagonist of the *bakufu*, invader of neighboring domains, occupier of the imperial city of *Kyoto* and the enemy of seafaring nations. Under the thirty-one year stewardship of Mori Takachika, the centuries-old Mori *han* will be dissolved, its noble house become a pariah in the nation of Japan, and the *Choshu* Domain absorbed into imperial holdings. A grim and painful future awaits the people of the *Choshu* Domain.

Chapter Sixteen
A Tour De Force

In January 1855 the U.S. Navy ships *Susquehanna, Mississippi, Powhatan, Allegheny* and escorts arrive in the Azores where they are met by another U.S. Navy ship, the *USS Supply*. The *Supply*, acquired by the Navy in 1846 and used in the Mexican War, is now a stores ship providing materials and supplies to other U.S. Navy ships on cruise. In the curious case of the Supply, she has been ordered to rendezvous with Commodore Perry's Squadron in the Azores for the purpose of said resupply, then to proceed to North Africa for a load of camels to be used by the U.S. Cavalry in the American Southwest.

Okada, Jiro and Takeshi, by now having learned some American *gaijin* sailor talk, watch and listen as officers from a half dozen anchored vessels arrive at the *Susquehanna* by longboat for an officer's conference. Among those attending is a twenty-five year Navy veteran from the *USS Mississippi*, Lieutenant David S. McDougal. The senior officers meet below deck and crowd around the green felt-covered wardroom table of the *Susquehanna* to hear the Commodore speak.

"Gentlemen, the Azores are our last resupply station before Philadelphia and the end of this cruise and mission. We have circumnavigated the globe using steam-powered vessels and opened the door to the closed-country of Japan. Many a shipwrecked and lost seaman may now be saved and receive fair treatment in the Japanese archipelago because of our efforts. Our merchant and naval vessels now have a new source of resupply, and most importantly for the future, trade may be extended between our nations. You, gentlemen, in this wardroom today, having participated in the mission, and having helped negotiate and secure the Convention of Kanagawa, have made this a reality. You are to be congratulated! A toast. A toast to our successful mission and to our safe arrival home!"

"To home and hearth. Cheers!" All join in.

On March 10, 1855 the *USS Susquehanna* arrives in port, Philadelphia. The officers and crew disembark as do the trio from Japan. Their conveyance, *USS Susquehanna* ends her naval career and is decommissioned the next month. Commodore Perry, suffering terribly from arthritis, soon retires, entering a race with death to complete his memoirs before he is taken. At dockside, Port of Philadelphia the trio is met by a young assistant to Secretary of State William L. Marcy, Thomas Bayard. Thomas is a young, up-and-coming Democrat, having recently entered U.S. State Department service. He will be the trio's teacher, minder and travel companion for the months to come. Thomas has prepared for his new assignment by wisely using the Portuguese language and its sources to cross-reference rudimentary Japanese. He locates and greets his new charges.

Bowing, Thomas says, "*Konnichiwa. Hajimemashite. Thomas de gozaimasu*, Good day. Pleased to meet you, I'm Thomas."

Okada speaks for the trio. "Good day, sir. My name is Okada, Tesuo. Here, my colleagues, Jiro and Takeshi." All bow. Thomas bows again.

"My carriage and a light wagon are here. Please follow me. We will ride the carriage to the railway station. The wagon will follow with your belongings."

Boarding the surrey, another first. None of the trio has ever sat in wheeled conveyance before other than a *jinrikusha*. The teamed-carriage moves away from the Navy Yard docks and the Delaware River onto Prime Street, first passing Swedes Church, Sparks' Shot Tower, and then the Children's Asylum on its way to the Baltimore and Ohio Railroad Station. Jiro comments as they "see" an American city for the first time.

"Unbelievable eh, Takeshi? The buildings are all made of brick or stone as are many of the streets as well. Carriages and wagons are everywhere. There are even wagons of people being pulled along parallel iron lines embedded in the street. Many buildings are belching black smoke from stacks. I wonder if they all have steam engines inside?"

"Steam engines inside the buildings? Why, Jiro? It can't be steam engines, it must be for heat. It's cold here!" Their carriage crosses several railroad tracks as they near the Baltimore and Ohio station.

"Look Takeshi, iron lines attached to wooden cross-beams which are not embedded in the stone streets. How do they move wagons down these lines, I wonder?"

137

"Gentlemen, we are approaching the Baltimore and Ohio Railroad station. We just passed over tracks for the trains. Have you never seen tracks or a train before?" asks Thomas.

Thomas' question is answered by silence. Tickets in hand, they board the train for Washington D.C. The one hundred-fifty mile trip will take about six hours with stops in Wilmington and Baltimore. The trio is amazed by the locomotives, rail lines, wires, bridges and factories. The scale of development is quite beyond their collective imaginations.

For six hours the B and O locomotive belches smoke and cinder clattering down its main line toward Washington, D.C. Okada, Jiro and Takeshi sit in a first class carriage, gawking, talking and lunching their way to the Capitol of the United States. By late afternoon the train begins its approach into the Baltimore and Ohio Union Station on Massachusetts Avenue, Washington, D.C. Here they again board a surrey, cross the roundabout at the intersection of California, Massachusetts and Delaware Avenues and head south passing the Senate Office Building and arriving at the U.S. Capitol Building. Although built in 1800, the beautiful, white neoclassical Capitol building is undergoing a major renovation and the yet unfinished addition of a huge rotunda dome. Stopping only for a quick look, they continue on, northwest on Pennsylvania Avenue to Willard's Hotel, near both the White House and the U.S. Treasury.

Thomas explains, "You will stay here for several days. Tomorrow, we will meet my boss, Secretary Marcy. It is possible that he may take you to call on the President, Franklin Pierce. You may take your meals in the dining room. Please be comfortable. I will arrange everything at the front desk."

"What do you mean they can't stay here?" asks Thomas, most astounded.

"No Chinamen allowed in the hotel, sir."

"They are not Chinamen! They are Japanese. They are official guests of the United States Government! I have reservations for them!" counters Thomas in a very agitated manner.

"Sorry, sir. No Jappers either. House rules. You may speak with Mr. Friedhof if you wish. He is the hotel manager. Mr. Willard is not available today."

"Very well then, Mr. Friedhof."

The front desk clerk disappears into a back room and after, what feels like an eternity to Thomas, a small, bespectacled, dapper-dressed Mr. Friedhof emerges. Before Friedhof can even introduce himself, Thomas breaks in.

"Now see here. I represent the United States State Department and these are my guests!"

"There, there. Calm yourself sir. I understand that there has been a misunderstanding. We will honor your reservations and do our best to meet your particular needs. Please, make no further demonstrations. I beg you sir."

Surprised, as well as a little embarrassed, but satisfied, Thomas begins to calm. Friedhof continues, "We have three adjoining rooms and a private bath at the end of the East Wing. These quarters should suit your guests quite nicely. Also, I will arrange for private dining off the main menu. This should provide a degree of privacy and comfort to your guests as well as keep them out of the public eye as to not cause alarm or further incident. Are these arrangements acceptable to you, Mr. errh?"

"Thomas, sir. Thomas Bayard, sir. United States State Department, assistant to Secretary Marcy.

"Ah, I see Mr. Bayard. Please give Secretary Marcy my regards."

"Thank you. Thank you again, sir."

Okada, Jiro and Takeshi are eventually escorted from the front desk to their third-floor rooms at the end of the hall. Their luggage is carried by Negro porters. Their satisfaction turns to joy when they are shown a private bath with hot water! The trio have not had a proper bath since departing Japan a year ago. They closely examine the copper, shoe-shaped tub with its cold water intake and hot water recirculation system. The idea has been lifted from Isaiah Rogers' Tremont Hotel designed "bathrooms" in Boston but now a feature at Willard's.

They sup in a private ante-chamber, more to isolate them from others, ladies and gentlemen of quality, rather than for their comfort. At this point in their *tour de force* of the United States, the distinction does not bother them. They are hungry! Unable to read the menu, they are assisted by a Negro waiter named Charles.

"These menu items are meats, sirs. Here is some beef, some pork and lamb. Down here are the seafood items. The house has a wonderful oyster stew…"

"Stew! No stew, please no stew," interjects Takeshi

"The gentlemen don't like stew, I take it. Our Maryland-style crabcakes are powerful good, specialty of the house. Asparagus and some creamed Bermuda onions perhaps?"

With no answer forthcoming, Charles takes his own suggestions, retrieves the menus and places the order with the kitchen. The trio is served tea.

The mouth-watering smell of Maryland-spiced shrimp and Maryland blue crab cakes drifts through the room as Charles returns with their food. The dishes are placed in the center of the table with serving spoons. Okada, Jiro and Takeshi each pull out their carefully preserved chopsticks and begin to pick the food out of the serving dishes without the benefit of the spoons.

"Oh, the gods are wonderful! These shrimp are so, so good. I do not recognize the spice, but they are very plump and tender," says Takeshi.

Jiro does not have much experience with shrimp but is eating them as fast as Takeshi. Okada samples a crab cake.

"*Oshii, oshii*, delicious, delicious," replies Jiro.

"Delicious. Really very delicious. For a year we suffered with shit for food, but this meal is fit for the gods," comments Okada between bites.

The next day, promptly at 9 A.M., Thomas meets and greets the trio in the public reception area. It is a fine day. Thomas cannot mask his excitement.

"This morning we will meet my boss, the Secretary of State, Marcy. After a brief introduction, we will proceed from the Treasury Building across the street to the White House. There you will meet President Franklin Pierce and enjoy a garden concert by The President's Own, the U.S. Marine Corps Band. Sounds good?"

"Yes, good, good," replies Okada.

At the Treasury, Secretary Marcy awaits their arrival. Marcy, a stern-looking man with bushy white eyebrows and a formal, high, starched, white collar reminds Jiro and Takeshi just a little of their *Yushima Seido* task master, Rector Sokan.

The Secretary meets and greets the trio. He displays some deference to Okaka, but speaks mainly in words the trio cannot understand and which Thomas cannot interpret. The meeting cannot end quickly enough. Exiting the Treasury Building, Thomas and the trio cross the newly cobblestoned Pennsylvania Avenue to the White House. They are met at the door and guided to the garden where the President is already seated waiting for his guests and for the concert to begin. Upon their arrival, the President stands, shakes each hand, bows slightly and sits. Thomas thanks God that no words are exchanged. Again, he doesn't have to interpret!

For several weeks in the spring of 1855, Thomas and the trio spend time in and around Washington, D.C., learning one another's language and customs. They visit the Smithsonian Institute, the Washington Navy Yard, the unfinished Washington monument and Congress. They ride carriage, trolley and trains. They wear Western clothes, learn the art of using the knife, spoon and fork. They eat Western cuisine, and even develop a taste for oyster "stew."

"There is no short way back to the Japans. We have planned the fastest route, a route that will provide you as much exposure to the Americas as possible. From Washington, you will again board the Baltimore and Ohio railroad. This time however it will take you west to Cincinnati, Ohio. In Cincinnati you will visit the Cincinnati Marine Works, a builder of river steamers. You will board the newly built *Natchez V* and steam downriver with the owner, Captain Thomas P. Leathers, from Cincinnati to Cairo, Illinois on the Ohio River, then from Cairo to New Orleans, Louisiana on the mighty Mississippi River. From New Orleans passage will be booked for you to Colón, Republic of Columbia."

"Columbia?" asks Okada. "Why we go to Columbia?"

"Exciting news, Okada. Only earlier this year, the Inter-Oceanic Railway was completed and opened for passengers. You three will be among the first in the world to travel from the Atlantic Ocean at Colón, across the Isthmus of Panama to Panama City on the Pacific Ocean. In Panama City passage will be booked for you on the Pacific Mail Steamship Company to San Francisco and then on to Japan. I don't know right now, whether the ship from San Francisco will be civilian or naval but it will be on the first available ship.

"How long this take?" asks Okada

"I'm not certain, Okada. Maybe ten to twelve weeks from Washington to Japan. Much faster than the year it took you to get here! I will escort you as far as Cincinnati. Any questions? I'm sure there are many but we'll have time to talk on the train. We depart tomorrow."

They travel westward on the B and O from Washington, first north to Baltimore and then west to Harper's Ferry, Grafton, Parkersburg, and finally Cincinnati, straight through the industrial heartland of America.

At the Cincinnati Marine Works, Thomas easily identifies the Captain in amongst the workmen in the yard. Captain Leathers is medium height, with an unruly shock of white hair, a heavy brow and a thick, full beard. He paces back and forth as though he were on deck.

"Good morning, Captain Leathers." Greets Thomas.

"Good morning, Mr. Bayard? I received your telegram. These are our guests, I presume?"

"Yes sir. May I introduce Messrs. Okada, Jiro and Takeshi from Japan."

The Japanese trio bow on cue. They have had a lot of practice.

"This is the *Natchez V*. She is three hundred feet long, has six boilers and can haul a load of four thousand four hundred cotton bales. She'll carry us to New Orleans in comfort and with speed. Let's get these gentlemen billeted aboard, we depart first light to-morrow morning," boasts Captain Leathers.

The Ohio River valley is beautiful as the Mississippi River valley is wide. For almost two weeks the trio travel with the current and under the watchful eye of Captain Leathers to New Orleans. In New Orleans, a telegram is waiting for the Captain, instructing him that the trio has been booked passage on a U.S. Mail Steamship Company boat to Colón. The ship departs in several days. Captain Leathers offers the use of the *Natchez V* as their home until that time.

One afternoon the trio decide to see the sights of the previously French, Cajun City of New Orleans. Unaccustomed to being unescorted, they mistakenly enter the wrong salon in search of an evening meal.

"You Chinamen, get your yella asses' outa here!" scolds the bartender.

"We not Chinamen, sir. We are Japanese," corrects Okada politely.

"I will not stand to be sassed by some uppity-ass Chinaman," exclaims the bartender, now furious at being corrected in front of his patrons.

"Japanese!" states Okada firmly.

The heavy-set Cajun bartender emerges from behind the bar and grabs Okada by the back of his shirt collar before he can react.

Okada is hustled across the floor and thrown out the front door with Jiro and Takeshi scurrying out just ahead. Okada bounces off the boardwalk and hits the packed dirt street hard, head first. Even Jiro and Takeshi can hear the crack when he hits. They rush to his side. Okada groans once or twice, and goes limp. His neck broken; Okada's unseeing eyes stare straight ahead. He is dead.

Eventually Captain Leathers arrives on the scene of dead Okada and the very distraught Jiro and Takeshi. Facts become twisted, words misunderstood, and even in multi-racial, and multi-cultural New Orleans there is no justice for a dead "Chinaman." No investigation will be conducted, no charges proffered. The unlucky Okada, a non-Caucasian, non-Christian is not accepted as fit for burial in consecrated Christian cemeteries. His pine-box coffin is hastily interned in the corner of a city plot reserved for paupers and nameless transients.

In shock from the death of Okada, Jiro and Takeshi embark on the *SS Falcon* en route from New York to Colón, Republic of Columbia via New Orleans and continue their journey, now south across the Gulf of Mexico. Only a year or so before, cross-Isthmus travelers were forced to endure a grueling, week-long expedition on foot or mule across hazardous, mosquito-infested jungle, river, swamp and lake to reach the Pacific-side town of Panama City. Jiro and Takeshi however board a new Inter-Oceanic Railway carriage and cross the Isthmus to Panama City in less than a day!

After the Okada incident, Jiro and Takeshi reserve their sightseeing to that which passes by the open window of their railway carriage. The province is poor and rebellious. Vestiges of Spanish heritage abound. The crumbling beauty of colonial architecture awes the travelers, but the language and appearance of the pitiable, mixed-race inhabitants induce yet another culture shock. The terminus of the Inter-Oceanic Railroad is a large combination railroad and ship pier jutting into the Gulf of Panama on the Pacific side. The duo disembark their railway carriage only to quickly re-embark the waiting Pacific Mail Steamship Company steamer, the *SS California*, for San Francisco, the next leg of their journey back to Japan.

Steaming with the Pacific current, the *SS California* makes good time to San Francisco. Even Jiro and Takeshi have become excited to see the gold-rush city by the bay. Their youth and curiosity overcome the trauma of losing of Okada. For one final week Jiro and Takeshi breath in and experience all that life offers in a place and a country they will never return to.

Jiro and Takeshi spend some happy hours camouflaged in the immensity of the Chinese presence and of boom-town rush of San Francisco. Without Okada's watchful eye, the young men eat, drink and "entertain" themselves until the last of their Tokugawan gold and silver are spent. Fortunate timing, they embark the *USS Savannah*, flagship of Commodore William Mervine's Pacific Squadron, and steam west toward Japan, never looking back.

Chapter Seventeen
The Navy

*A*t age twenty, David S. McDougal reports aboard the aging *USS Congress* berthed at Norfolk, Virginia. The *USS Congress* is one of six, thirty-eight gun frigates authorized by Congress in the Naval Act of 1794. She has enjoyed a varied career; first in a squabble with France, then sailed twice against Mediterranean Barbary pirates, distinguished herself in high-seas conflict with Britain in the War of 1812, cruised South America and visited Chinese ports. Finally, for lack of repair materials and money, the *USS Congress* is berthed at Norfolk Naval Yard as a receiving ship for naval recruits.

"Good morning and welcome aboard the *USS Congress*, Midshipman recruits that you are. I am Chief Petty Officer Pautzke. I will be your mother aboard 'my' ship. Forget anything you have learned in life thus far. I will teach you to eat, shit, dress and carry out your assigned duties. You and you alone are my mission on this ship and I, well, I am the flotsam upon which you hang. Learn to swim quickly little fish or you will certainly die.

"Now you will see Petty Officer Shubert here. He will record your names on the ship's register, have you sign the Articles of War and see that hammocks, uniforms, and necessaries are issued to you. You will be instructed in customs, etiquette, discipline, and basic seamanship before being transferred to your first ship. Make the most of what we have to offer and you will suffer little. Have any of you ever been aboard a boat before?" queries Chief Pautzke.

David raises his hand. "Yes, sir. I have repaired, refitted and sailed a ketch."

"A ketch? Refitted and sailed have you? Well, in this man's navy you will need to do more than hang a bedsheet on a raft and call yourself a sailor. Petty Officer Shubert, they are yours!"

The first days aboard the Congress are anything but tedium. New mates to befriend or learn to avoid, new schedules and routines to learn, David takes a moment to write a note home.

Dear Mother and Father,

I have safely arrived at the Norfolk Naval Yard and reported aboard the receiving ship, USS Congress. It is an old frigate tied up to the pier which serves as a floating school for both Midshipman and seaman recruits alike. We won't cruise with her, as she needs to be towed when moved. I suspect we'll be here some weeks, before being assigned to a regular Navy ship upon which I will begin my three year hitch as Midshipmen.

So far the schedule is not too trying and the lessons not too difficult. I miss your cooking for sure Ma and I miss being able to ask Pa a question without being belittled or demeaned. I will learn to become a proper Navy man and make you all proud. I am satisfied with my decision to enlist, and know that time, application and patience will be bear fruit.

Sincerely,
Your devoted son, David

P.S. Ma, if you ever see Katie Kowalski about town, please extend my regards!

During David's stint aboard the *Congress*, new recruits arrive daily as do sailing orders for those having completed their on-board training. After three months, the awaited orders arrive and Midshipman David S. McDougal is reassigned to the *USS John Adams*, an old frigate serving out its final years as part of the West Indies Squadron. The *USS John Adams*, like the *USS Congress*, is one of the six thirty-eight gun frigates built in accordance with the Naval Act of 1794. Unlike the *Congress*, the *Adams* continues to ply the seas, albeit close to home, interdicting West Indian pirates and chasing tax-evading rum runners and smugglers. The happy times aboard David's first ship end after only twelve months. The *Adams*, old and tired, is ordered back to Norfolk where she will be almost entirely rebuilt before reentering service in 1831. Requiring only a skeleton crew, the fresh Midshipman is reassigned to newer ship, the *USS Warren*, a sloop of war carrying twenty guns. After undergoing minor repairs in Norfolk, the Warren sails south to Brazil Station, an ad hoc squadron of United States naval vessels protecting commence, interdicting the slave trade and enforcing the Madison Doctrine even south of the equator. Master Commandant Benjamin Cooper is David's commander aboard the Warren.

"McDougal, even as a Midshipman you must prepare yourself for the day when you will command a ship. Therefore I want you to work this navigation problem in addition to your regular watch. We have been ordered south in order to shepherd American-flagged merchantmen in and around the Brazilian coast. Old Emperor Pedro of Brazil was soundly beaten by the Argentinians in a recent border dispute, but it's still a blood feud and these are dangerous waters. Plot a course to Port of Spain, Sao Luis, Rio de Janeiro, and Montevideo," orders Commandant Cooper.

"Aye, sir. Trinidad, the coast of Brazil and Uruguay it is, sir."

David reflects, "Brazil Station will take us well away the West Indies patrol area. We may be afloat for months, a year or more perhaps. Port of Spain is my last chance to post a letter to Katherine."

That night, distracted and taking a short break from his navigation problem, David inks a short letter to Katherine Kowalski. Placing his writing paper atop his nautical charts and notes, under the light then shadow, shadow then light of swinging lantern above the table, David writes to the object of his private intentions.

Dear Katherine,

It has been some months since I last saw you in Leonard-stown, then again only twice since I left to join the Navy more than two years ago. I hope that you fondly remember me? Leaving Leonardstown, I feel as though the sea beckons me and that the Navy will be my vocation. Though far away from my boyhood home, in this small lamp-lit cabin below deck of a ship of war, your fond memory remains with me, here in my heart. I know that we are different. I, the son of an immigrant working man, you the daughter of an established, freeholding family of means. Yet, Katherine, I have ambition and potential. I have potential to become someone important, someone who can make a difference, someone bigger than Leonardstown, Maryland.

I hope that you will receive this letter in the manner in which it was intended. In my quiet and personal time, I have wondered if you might not have given some notice of me? If so, would you then, allow me to call on you when I am next home on furlough? I should have, by then, taken my examination for lieutenant. I am sure you will be most impressed.

I look forward to your letter by return and any encouragement which you are able to give. Until we meet again Katherine.

Your servant, David

P.S. You may post your letter to Midshipman David S. McDougal, USS John Adams, homeport Norfolk Virginia. I should receive your letter, eventually.

Rumors of American fishing vessels and whalers being taken and converted into pirate vessels, carry the Adams south past Montevideo, Uruguay and the Argentine coast toward the settlement of Puerto Soledad in the far off Malvinas Islands. Master Commandant Cooper and the *USS John Adams* set a direct course to the Malvinas but are preempted by Captain Silas Duncan, commanding the *USS Lexington*, who not only locates four commandeered American vessels, but engages in a furious firefight with seal-hunting pirates.

"Damn Duncan's hide. That pirate den was ours for the taking, not Duncan's!" curses Master Commandant Cooper.

"Does it matter, sir? The pirates are either dead or captured, and soon to be hung. The ships can be returned to their rightful owners and the colonists of Puerto Soledad can resume their lives," asks David innocently.

"Ah, to be a Midshipman again. No Midshipman McDougal, it is not all right and it isn't that simple. Duncan gets mention in diplomatic posts. Duncan cleans out a nest of pirates and restores American property with no loss of life save a few scurvy scum eking out a living butchering seals on a God-forsaken, desolate shore in the south Atlantic. Duncan, the *Lexington* and crew get a battle star, if not literally, then figuratively. Duncan is viewed favorably by the Navy board for promotion. The *USS John Adams* gets nothing! In time you will learn that battles are fought at sea, on land and within the ranks of Navy. Do not forget this lesson, Midshipman McDougal!"

"Aye sir, within the ranks of the Navy. I better understand now," replies David, still clearly puzzled by Cooper's verbal venom toward Duncan and the Lexington.

In addition to clearing Puerto Soledad of pirates, the Lexington evacuates two or more score of emaciated, worn-out colonists and repatriates them to Buenos Aires. The Malvinas, first French, then Spanish, then British, then Argentine Spanish again, is quickly reoccupied and garrisoned by the British not to be lost again. The remaining seal hunters and fisherman become a part of the Empire and grow to accept British colonial administration of the Falkland Islands.

In 1845 newspaperman John O'Sullivan coined the term Manifest Destiny. It was not an official policy of the United States Government, but was certainly on the minds of those in Congress who annexed the new Republic of Texas in 1846. In spite of Texas Revolution of 1836, the Centralist Republic of Mexico still considered Texas as sovereign Mexican territory. The opposing positions taken by the United States and Mexico were a recipe for war, a war that both sides were more than eager wage.

The war with Mexico is still raging as Lieutenant David S. McDougal reports aboard the *USS Mississippi* for duty. The *Mississippi* is a newer steam-powered paddle ship, laid down in Philadelphia in 1839, and whose construction was supervised by Commodore Matthew Perry, the father of the steam-powered Navy. David is pleased to finally be aboard a modern warship, a ship to soon see real action against a belligerent of his United States.

As Second Officer, David is effectively third in command of the *USS Mississippi*. Commodore Perry using the *Mississippi* as his flagship of the so-called Mosquito Squadron enforces a blockade of eastern Mexican ports. Later, the squadron bombards, supporting the famous amphibious assault of Veracruz.

"Commodore Perry, may I present my Second Officer, David McDougal."

"Captain Salter, thank you. Lieutenant McDougal, a pleasure I am sure. Where have you served prior to this ship, McDougal?" queries Perry.

"Thank you, Commodore. As you would expect, sir, I have served in various capacities as a Midshipman and Lieutenant aboard the *USS Warren* and *John Adams*," replies David.

"The *Warren* and *Adams*? Relics! Relics, McDougal. Those ships were based on British designs from Revolutionary times and laid down by order of the Congress in 1794! This ship now, a steam-powered warship with modern guns and explosive ordnance, this is the future. Don't forget it, Lieutenant. Steam-power is the key to the Navy in this century!"

The *Mississippi* steams south to rejoin the Mosquito Squadron blockading eastern Mexico. Other ships join with an amphibious force under the command of General Winfield Scott and his staff aide, Captain Robert E. Lee. The Mosquito Squadron lays down a devastating naval gun fire barrage and the fortress of Veracruz which is carried and secured. As the land forces press on toward the Mexican capitol of Mexico City, Commodore Perry and his Mosquito Squadron languish in the, now backwaters of the conflict off Veracruz ferrying supplies and replacements for the land forces and receiving a harvest of wounded and dead from another unnecessary and murderous war.

With the smell of the guns lingering in his nostrils, David now sees the human waste of war. Scores of wounded lie on deck, their suffering compounded by the sun, humidity and flies. The dead which either arrive dead or die onboard begin to bloat, putrefy and reek before they can be ferried out to deeper waters of the Bahia de Campeche for burial at sea. Trying to be discreet, David walks with a handkerchief in hand. He leaves his quarters, the wardroom or quarterdeck only when necessary.

"Let us leave this wretched place before we either are roasted under this damned sun, or die of pestilence brought aboard by these Marines," says David quietly, but not quietly enough, to another junior officer. Captain Salter, aware of poor morale amongst the crew, reprimands his Lieutenant on the spot.

"Mister McDougal. Uncalled for! Your personal feelings on the state of affairs aboard this ship are of no interest to anyone. You will carry out your duties in a professional manner and refrain from further commentary on other matters. Do I make myself clear, sir!" snaps Captain Salter.

"Aye, aye sir. My apologies, sir" responds David, angry with himself for being overheard. He discreetly retreats to his quarters, brooding.

Generalissimo Antonio de Padua Maria Severino Lopez de Santa Anna y Perez de Lebron is ultimately defeated and driven into exile in Kingston, Jamaica. Commodore Perry's ad hoc Mosquito Squadron lifts its blockade of Mexican ports and disbands. The

Mississippi and Lieutenant McDougal, after a brief respite in homeport and furlough respectively, receive orders to cruise the Mediterranean, where, among other events, they carry the deposed King of Hungary, Lajos Kossuth, into exile.

Finally, in 1854, after his promotion and being awarded his first command, the *USS Warren*, Commander David S. McDougal writes, the now widowed Katherine (Kowalski) Griffiths a heartfelt letter asking for her hand in marriage.

> *Dear Katherine,*
>
> *More than two decades ago, a young boy left his home in Maryland, moved by a calling to serve his country and the chance to sail the seemingly endless seas. In the intervening years this boy has grown into a man, a man respected by many and travelled the world over. He has seen much of what the world has to offer, as well as the dark and ugly side of man, his earthly kingdoms and his shame.*
>
> *This man, of course, is I, David. In my experiences, upon the seas and in foreign lands, I remain a vessel half-filled, desiring to share myself and my life's treasures with a woman who will accept me unconditionally, as I will accept her.*
>
> *Dear Katherine, you have always held a place in my heart. My own selfish pride, circumstance and time would have it that I should remain a bachelor all these*

years and that you would marry, bear a child and become a widow. Still to me, it is as though you have never changed, only I. I had to undergo these years of change and maturing in order to become acceptable to you. Could you consider me as a partner and husband? Might you give just consideration to this, a proposal of marriage?

If you would accept my proposal, then I will, at first opportunity, take furlough and return for that happy day. If you cannot find it in your heart to say yes, then I thank you sincerely for always having been an object of affection in my heart and for the tender care you provided to mother during her illness and until her death. I look forward to your reply with great hope and trepidation.

Yours most affectionately, David

Since the day David happened on the "Ketch of the Day" until now, a blue water naval Commander with his first command, and from young manhood until a middle-aged bachelor, now to become a married man, the year 1852 brings great change to the life of Commander David S. McDougal. But it is the next ten years that will present David with his greatest challenges, joys and disappointments of his lifetime.

Chapter Eighteen
Lord of the Chosbu Domain

The traditional one hundred days of mourning have passed since the surprise and untimely death of Lord Mori Narimoto. Young Takachika is young Takachika no more. He is become the thirteenth Lord Mori, Prince of *Nagato*, Lord of the *Choshu* Domain.

In an upper chamber of *Hagi* Castle, a half-dozen *daijin* of the domain gather. Ikeda, the leading member of the *daijin* kneels before Takachika and holds out the revered swords of the *han*.

"My lord, I present to you *biboujintsukuri*, the widow-maker, sword and its little brother," proclaims Ikeda.

A centuries-old *katana* and *tanto* are passed to Takachika. These swords, more than anything, are the symbol of his position and clan. Having respectfully received the swords, he slowly and carefully slides each from its scabbard, almost lovingly inspects the silver-blue polished metal, fingers the inscriptions, admires the razor-sharp edges and replaces them in their respective scabbards. The honor and responsibility of the *han* has passed to him.

Takachika conducts a ritual tea ceremony to serve his honored guests, mainly *daijin* of the domain, witnesses to his ascension to the hereditary position of leader of the Mori *han*. Those in attendance are seated on *zabuton*, sitting *seiza*, erect, looking forward with their hands on their knees. Takachika carefully spoons the green tea powder into a ceramic bowl, then pours steaming hot water into the powder, stirring it with a bamboo whisk. When the tea is prepared, Takachika first passes the bowl to the leading member of the *daijin*, who carefully turns the bowl in his hands to the right three times then gracefully sips a little tea. Passing the bowl to the next *daijin* the ceremonial process is repeated.

Finally, like he has done so many times before, but with special significance on the forty-ninth and hundredth days since the passing of his father, Takachika honors his ancestral dead with candles, incense and prayer. All these rituals being scrupulously observed, he can now turn his attentions to matters of the domain, and more importantly, his personal desire for revenge against those who tried to assassinate him on the *Tokaido* Road.

"Takahashi! Come let us speak," orders Lord Mori. Lord Mori and Counselor Takahashi closet themselves in private chambers.

"Takahashi, you shall continue to serve as Counselor, as it pleases me."

"Yes *tono*, I only live to serve you," replies Counselor Takahashi automatically.

"You will, of course, assist me with audiences today and every day, but more importantly we must exact our revenge on those dogs from *Yedo* who attempted to have me killed. I understand

Jedo is a good man for such unsavory tasks, summon him!" demands Takachika.

"Jedo has not been seen in some time my lord. He has disappeared. Your father tried unsuccessfully to have him located, but to no avail. Explain to me your wishes my lord, then I will find the right men and your will shall be carried out," answers Takahashi straight-faced without betraying a hint of knowledge of the true whereabouts of the months-dead Jedo.

"I suspect *bakufu* agents in *Okayama*, no doubt with the assistance of Utako, the eighth lord of *Okayama*, had a hand in the act. But we, the Mori will set it straight. It is not a question of what we will do, it is a question of how we shall do it!"

Counselor Takahashi contemplates his delicate and complex assignment. He knows that the *bakufu* had no hand in the attempt on Takachika's life, but at the same time has no particular goodwill in his heart for the Shogun dictator in *Yedo* or his bureaucracy. Hostage taking by the *bakufu* is one thing, but retaliatory assassination is another. Still, a strong, decisive leader could be good for the domain and his failure to please would certainly lead to his dismissal, disgrace, even death.

The Counselor considers his options. "It is best to appear compliant even diligent in my duties." Having decided for himself, he replies. "We shall employ a core of *yohei ninja*, mercenary assassins, who in turn can school others from within the *han*. This should please and satisfy my Lord Mori." Again, for himself he concludes, "Concurrently, however, I will begin to develop contacts with the *bakufu* through Takazawa Yoshio in *Shikimi*. *Yedo* should be advised that the 13th *daimyo* of the Mori *han*, is headstrong, possibly dangerous and warrants watching."

In the following months, gold and servant girls attract just the type of men Takachika seeks. The impertinent leader of the group of *yohei ninja* is Ito, a skilled and cunning man with a passion for refined butchery. He is highly organized and diligent but is prone to debauched distraction. As he and his men train, they accept a number of selected men from the ranks of Lord Mori's foot soldiers.

As Ito and his men train, Lord Mori selects three men to lead his land and sea forces: Mori Masamitsu, his uncle and obvious choice for overall command; Akane Takito, an accomplished cavalryman; and Tamura Saburo, a fisherman, smuggler, sometime pirate who will captain his fleet. Such activities require money, and money is raised by "regulating" sea-borne traffic through the *Shimonoseki Straits* and Tamura's efforts at sea off the *Ryukyu Islands*. Lord Mori, with forethought, uses these activities to raise his profile and leverage his importance among constantly competing *daimyo*.

Counselor Takahashi is inwardly alarmed by the aggressive and belligerent nature of these activities. At great risk to his person, he begins sending more regular reports to *Yedo* via *Shikimi*.

Initially, alarm in *Yedo* is muted. For centuries the Shogunate has ruled Japan through a loose confederation of the *daimyo*. Powerful *daimyo* can make powerful friends; of course, the opposite can also be true. In most cases, "voluntary" hostage holding, as was to be the case with young Takachika, and bribery usually manage to keep the more unruly *daimyo* in check. Using this logic, the *bakufu* arrange for gifts, courtesy of their new American contacts, gifts of modern cannon to "protect" the *Shimonoseki Straits* and smaller, surplus steam-powered vessels to patrol the waters nearby.

Given the perceived threat, Counselor Takahashi is puzzled by the Shogunate reaction to his covert messages. The *bakufu* have provided potentially lethal gifts and are seemingly indifferent to the threat. Now he pauses to consider his exposure, and immediately greatly limits his future communications lest he be identified as a source of information. He feels alone.

Although he does not realize it, Lord Mori begins to develop a military doctrine of asymmetric warfare. His powerful conventional forces of infantry, artillery, cavalry and ships will deter potential enemies' overt actions or reactions, while his pocket force of *yohei ninja* are able to carry out pinpoint actions against those who would oppose him and incite fear. Unbeknownst to Lord Mori, "his" doctrine was first effectively developed and employed by the ancient Parthians two thousand years before.

Military preparedness notwithstanding, the heartbeat of the domain and the strength upon which it is measured is rice. The lifecycle of the domain is planting, harvesting and replanting. Bounty or starvation is measured by a *koku* of rice, one *koku* being enough rice to feed one person for one year. When the lord of the manor is resident, court is held daily. All adjudication rests with the lord of the domain.

Lord Mori Takachika's daily routine is most influenced by three factors: first, the Imperial Decree of *Joi Jikko No Chokumei*, revere the Emperor and expel the foreigners; second, his permanent hatred of the Shogunate; and three, abusing servant girls. He justifies many of his actions by this Imperial Edict and looks to the *Mikado*, the Emperor, to rule directly by decree. He sees the Shogunate as illegitimate and corrupt, interfering with the rightful rule of the *daimyo*. Finally, as undisputed ruler of his fief, his primary distraction and entertainments are his carnal inclinations with any number of servant or peasant girls, young or younger, married or not, with whom he can pleasure. Though not a poor administrator, his focus tends toward the destabilization of the existing Shogunate order, belligerency toward non-allied domains, and pleasures of this world.

Months in preparation, Lord Mori Takachika's first direct action is to exact a measure of revenge from what he sees as the Shogunate's attempt on his life on the *Tokaido* Road. Enabled and assisted by a cowered Counselor Takahashi, Lord Mori orders Ito and a number of his *yohei ninja* into action.

"Ito-kun, you will proceed with your men to *Okayama* by stealth. Go where the ragged people go, blend in. There you will identify, follow and observe agents of the *bakufu.* As you are able, eliminate one each day for a week. Dispose of them, or pieces of them in conspicuous places in and around *Okayama* Castle. I want to send a clear message to both Utako and the *bakufu.* First to Utako, he should be careful which horse he rides. Second to the *bakufu,* we will not be intimidated or bribed into submission. Leave no trace, this too will give them all something to think about for a short while. Now go!" orders Lord Mori.

Within a fortnight the first of the seven deeds is done. A young customs official of the *bakufu* is followed then slaughtered on a side street after an evening out at a teahouse. His young body is hung upside down from a tree near the confluence of the moat and the main gate of *Okayama* Castle. His entrails have been pulled through the gaping hole once occupied by his head and neck. So no mistake can be made as to his identity, his head is stuck on a stick nearby, with his severed cock in his mouth.

Ito, more efficient than Jedo, practices his art night after night for five more days. *Okayama* is in a near state of panic in that rumors abound and facts are few. Only the officials have concluded that these messy, public murders are not the work of a madman, rather politically inspired and directed assassinations. News quickly finds its way back to *Hagi* Castle. Lord Mori is elated. Counselor Takahashi, the only person outside of Ito's select group to be privy to the general plan to take a measure of revenge, is in a state of shock. Officials, retainers and peasants of the *Choshu* Domain wait for more news with mixed curiosity, horror and fear.

On the seventh night Ito himself is duped. One of his group has already been quietly killed, another detained. Ito is lead to a location, not of his choosing, by his intended victim. Instead of catching his prize unaware, he is surrounded by Utako's men and captured along with two others. In the melee, Ito turns on himself and attempts a suicide. He is unsuccessful. Bound, hooded and dragged, Ito is taken deep to within the center of *Okayama* Castle. He is thrown into a cold, stone-floored room, without natural light. There he lies for what seems to be several days. Unable to move due to his restraints, he can only wait or die. His appendages go numb, he urinates and defecates on himself. In his mind, he is already dead, but no, within minutes of the first round of torture, he will understand that he is still very much alive.

At *Hagi* Castle the daily flow of news from far off *Okayama* suddenly dries up. Lord Mori can only imagine that Ito has finished his work and has disappeared. He will surely take a circuitous route back and may not reappear for some time. Still, the lack of closure or news of an investigation by the *bakufu* are a cause for concern if not alarm.

In the bowels of Okayama Castle, Utako's man confronts his victim, Ito.

"I don't think I've ever smelled a *ninja* quite as ripe as you. You consider yourself a *ninja*, I suppose? Does our *ninja* friend have a name? From where do you hail? No name, no home? In any case, time will reveal all secrets. Trust me, I should know. This is my vocation, to help you remember, to uncover secrets. Yes my friend, you are going to die. But then, ultimately, we all die. Your choice is how you will die. Shall you die quickly or do you wish to die more slowly, over several days perhaps. Tell me. I will help you," states Ito's tormentor, Utako's executioner, matter of factly.

"So, let us loosen your tongue. Shall we begin with your fingers? Your toes? Your skin? So many choices. But I promise you, I will not take your tongue. I want to hear you scream. I want to hear you beg. And finally, I want to hear you speak!" continues the executioner.

In the end, Ito's strength and determination are of no consequence. The executioner has already learned all he needs to know from Ito's other two men. They are dead, of course. The executioner is simply practicing his vocation and enjoying Ito's torment.

"These men are from the *Choshu* Domain, my Lord Utako. They were sent to target *bakufu* officials. No doubt to send a message to *Yedo* and to embarrass you, my lord," reports the executioner. "The two underlings have been disposed of locally, but their leader, Ito, has been returned to *Hagi* Castle in very small pieces except his head which has a note stuck in his mouth."

"A note?"

"Yes, my lord. The message advises Lord Mori that we know from whence his man came, why he came and who he, errh, was."

"And the message?"

"Yes, my lord. The message reads: Here is Ito. Hound of Mori. His mission failed, but his hand revealed."

"Very good. That should stir things up a bit at *Hagi* Castle, eh?"

"Yes, my Lord Utako. Just a bit."

At *Hagi* Castle, Lord Mori is dumbstruck. Ito's covert mission has failed, and his hand has been revealed. He can expect serious retaliation, but when and from where? He is so angry with Ito, with himself. Two or three girls may make him feel better tonight.

Chapter Nineteen
A Big Man

To most in Albany and certainly within the firm of Vanderhornt, Klatt and Becht, Robert is a hero. He has not only
prevailed but combined detective and legal diligence into a dra-
matic courtroom revelation and victory. Naturally, there are de-
tractors, who, in spite of the evidence and testimony, had already
passed judgment and condemned the young immigrant brothers,
and who are bitter toward Robert for their defense and acquittal.
Still, the recently returned native son has earned due notice in
Albany, notice which will quickly develop in respect and pride.

After three short years of apprenticeship, Robert is prepared
and stands for the bar in the State of New York. He is successful.

"Three years ago our firm welcomed a young graduate of
Rutgers College into our firm. Today, our firm welcomes a colleague and New York's newest attorney at law," announces Mr.
Vanderhornt to the assembled company of Vanderhornt, Klatt
and Becht upon Robert's return.

"Thank you, sir, and all for your kind encouragement. I will try to make myself worthy of your trust and praise," responds Robert.

Like everywhere in the nascent republic, social and political fissures run close to the surface in 1839; New York is no exception. Tensions run high in the state which by virtue of its thriving commercial center, ports, railroads, rivers and canals attracts tens of thousands of immigrants, and free blacks, including many with religious affiliations other than the Protestant mainstay of post-colonial America. Robert, a noted university man now practicing law, a man with civic and political intentions, a company-grade officer in the New York State Militia, catches the eye of New York's new pro-immigrant, anti-slavery governor, the Honorable William Henry Steward.

Dear Mr. Pruyn

May I offer my belated, but sincerest congratulations of your pro bono defense in the O'Malley brothers' case last year. It is so very important, that we, as Christian men, in this God-given republic never forget that we all arrived here on these shores as immigrants, and that our Creator demands that we treat the least and marginalized in our society with dignity and respect. You sir have demonstrated your love of the Gospel and yourself as a true disciple of Christ as commanded and written in Matthew 25:40, "Because you did it to the least of these my brothers, you did it to me."

It would truly be a pleasure to meet a kindred spirit like yourself and to discourse on many matters of popular concern to the State of New York and these United States.

I do hope that you will accept this, my invitation, to lunch with me here at the Governor's Mansion at your earliest convenience.

Very Sincerely, William Henry Steward. Governor

Consummated with a one hour lunch of oysters, lamb, and creamed vegetables, Robert Pruyn and William Henry Steward begin a life-long friendship and collaboration which only ends with Steward's death in 1872. In his quiet, underdog manner, which is rapidly becoming his trademark, Robert heartily shakes the hand of New York's governor and thanks him for lunch.

"Thank you, Governor Steward. The lunch was delicious and your words are most encouraging," thanks Robert. Adding his "patented" and disarming line, he continues, "I will try to make myself worthy of your trust and praise."

"That's the attitude my boy. Keep up that attitude and **you'll** someday be governor!"

Robert accepts the praise and compliment in stride and returns to the office as though nothing noteworthy has happened this day.

Politically, Robert, a stable and conservative-tending man, sees his beloved republic in a turmoil of conflicting movements. In the founding days of the republic, Democrats and Federalism held sway. Gradually Federalism gave way to the Whig Party as the balancing second in the two-party system. The Whigs, being namesake to the American Whigs of 1776, an early independence group. In spite of notable American leaders such as Daniel Webster, Henry Clay, Generals William Henry Harrison and Zachary Taylor and Winfield Scott, the Whigs are rife of late with internal divisions on how to deal with the issue of slavery in the territories. The Democrats advocate "sovereignty" of the people. The Whigs stand for an unchanging Constitution and the "rule of law" which must protect minority voices in the midst of a "tyranny" of majority opinion. Add to this volatile mix, a nativist movement of American-born, white Protestant men demanding curbs in immigration and naturalization. The nativists see America being inundated by a flood of German and Irish Catholics as well as black freedmen.

In the City Council of Albany, Robert sees his chance to influence civic life by the "rule of law." So, as a nominal Whig, Robert enters politics for the first time and finds the experience invigorating, yet trying. The prominence of the Pruyn family, a solicitous father, Robert's connections as a local attorney and State Militia officer, all serve to make him a perfect candidate when, a year later, in 1841 Governor Steward appoints Robert as Solicitor General of the New York State Militia.

Robert's appointment as Solicitor General now gives him state-wide recognition and an official presence, which he later leverages into multiple election victories to the New York State Assembly, Albany County, 3rd District. He serves his terms as a Whig but remains painfully aware that his chosen political party is in decline and the day will come when new affiliation decisions may have to be made.

"What bothers me most is not necessarily the decline and ultimate demise of the Whig Party, but the ascendancy of the nativists. The Native American Party is a joke!" laments Robert to William Steward.

"That's why it's called the Know Nothing Party, Robert," jokes Governor Steward

"But it is an embarrassment to New York! Its headquarters there in New York City, the grandest city in all the United States. New York, the gateway city to America and a new way of life. And it is there where they are stirring up trouble, rioting against innocent immigrants even though their own forefathers were immigrants. I've never understood the rationale behind hating Catholics just because their bishop resides in Rome. The good, white, Anglo-Saxon Anglican bishop resides in Canterbury, yet the same people don't seem to hate him. It all makes about as much sense as calling Jews 'Christ killers,'" continues Robert.

"There, there. Calm yourself, Robert. There are many forces at work in our new country. Think about it: the Monroe Doctrine, Manifest Destiny, slavery, abolition, immigration and temperance, just to name a few. The country is developing in fits and spurts, there is much opportunity but there is also much friction. It is true that our old Whig Party may not be up to the task of meeting all these challenges, but a new party will surely take its place, and it won't be the Know Nothing Party! Constitutionalism, the rule of law and the universal rights of man are governance principals which transcend our tired, old Party," consoles the Governor.

"Well, if you say so, sir. I'll just watch you, and jump when you jump. You are so much more politically astute than I," concedes Robert.

Between the years 1848 and 1854 Robert serves six terms in the State Assembly, as well as two stints as Speaker pro tempore. Robert's close friend and ally, William Henry Steward, moves from the New York State Governor's Residence to national office. First elected in 1849, Steward, using his highly activist record of universal rights, abolitionism and temperance during his terms as governor, captures a seat in the United States Senate, initially as a Whig, and again later as a nascent Republican in 1855. Robert watches Steward's ascendant political career with amazement.

Although Robert's close friend Steward no longer resides in the Governor's Residence, his successor and fellow Whig, Myron Clark, does and he, though not a confidant of Robert, is no less impressed with Robert's intellect and hard work than was Steward. In his first year as Governor, Clark appoints Robert Adjutant General of the New York State Militia.

In less than twenty years' time, Robert has proven himself in apprenticeship, as an attorney, a military judge, a city council member, a state assemblyman, Assembly Speaker, and now a general officer in the New York State Militia. Robert, modest about his own laurels, closely watches and maintains a close relationship with his friend and fellow Republican, Senator William Henry Steward in Washington D.C. Someday soon Robert will follow him onto the national stage.

Chapter Twenty
Not of this World

*I*n the days following her wedding, but before the death of her father-in-law Lord Mori Narimoto, Chizuru comes to accept her surroundings and her fate. She is sometimes called to an official function, a meal or an event of importance to the *han* or the gods, but generally she is left alone in her private suite within the confines of *Hagi* Castle. As a "married" woman, she feels secure from other men with whom she may have infrequent contact, even her father-in-law. As a girl, not yet an adult, she feels somewhat safe from the ravaging of her husband, in that, the self-same father-in-law who attempted to rape her prior to her wedding, will demand that his son observe proprieties and not consummate the arranged marriage or molest her until she comes of age. It is an interesting conundrum, but it provides her with some peace and security nevertheless.

Chizuru's days are simple, her routine rarely varies. She rises early, bathes, dresses simply and prays at the Mori family shrine.

Not having been instructed by dogmatic Jesuits priests or evangelizing Franciscan friars and having been raised Shinto-Buddhist, she does not bear the burden of Christian religious boundaries. She kneels before the Mori family Shinto shrine, a shrine representing a collection of small deities governed by the solitary god, "one of the first to inhabit the high plain of the earth," rings the bell attached to a thick red and white rope, claps her hands once and prays:

> *Onze vader die in die hemel ziht*
> *Uw naam worde geheligd.*

"Mysterious are you my Creator. I do not begin to understand. I know only that which you have placed in my heart, that which calls me toward you and speaks to me. I do not ask for favor or reward, I ask only to know you. I have accepted my fate, reveal to me my purpose. I am Japanese, but I know that you created all men and that I, just as all creation, am important to you. Do not forsake me, my God. Amen."

Satisfied with her morning prayer, a prayer similar to her every morning prayer, she returns to her suite where she breakfasts and prepares for the day. With Chizuru, in her isolation, are several maiden servants who provide for her needs. Like her, they too were chosen and had little opportunity to express their preferences or desires. The young servant girls hail from poor families desperate to rid themselves of an expensive and useless female liability. They are considered fortunate to have entered the House of Mori for service.

In only a short time, however, the maidens and their lady have grown exceptionally close. Even at the risk of a spy being among them, Chizuru has shared with them her visions and her *kami*. She is beyond fear, for her *kami* will not forsake her.

"I felt as though death were upon me. I had no feeling, no pain. Remembering, it seems as though I could see and hear, yet all was blurred in a misty fog. I was lost and confused. At the moment of my confusion, I saw my *kami*. I recognized my Creator even before I heard its voice speak to me. I believe that I recognized it because I am part of its creation. My *kami* comforted me in a way I cannot explain. A deep peace descended upon me even as I awoke feeling my diseased body again. I felt my heartbeat, a cold sweat and involuntary tears welling up in my eyes. I no longer have anxiety or fear. But I long to know my purpose. This has been withheld from me. I pray to know my purpose every day, at the shrine. I close my eyes, knell, hold tight the symbol of the God of the Cross and pray. My *kami* speaks but only that it is with me. I am unable to transcend my own earthly desires, therefore my purpose has not been revealed to me." Confesses Chizuru.

"Oh, my lady, such a revelation. I long for your god to love me too!" gushes a lady.

"All of us here are children of the Creator. All of us are as important as the other. Do not envy me, my *kami*. It is a source of joy but also frustration. It is a joy in the sense that I have seen my God. It is a frustration in the sense that I cannot overcome my own human selfishness and desires to understand my God."

"My lady, it is forbidden to speak of the God of the Cross. You must be careful," cautions another of her ladies.

"Careful for your sakes, for the sake of my family in *Shikimi* perhaps, but I do not fear for myself."

"We are yours, my lady. Help us move beyond our earthly desires to that which is not of this world. Bless us, my lady. God works through you."

Though not yet of age, but as expected, Chizuru is summoned by Lord Mori. Her maiden servants prepare her for the moment in every way. She enters into Lord Mori's private chamber, bows and submits herself to him. In the beginning, he does not seem to grasp a difference beyond his own carnal desires. He believes that her lack of responsiveness, the absence of any sort of pleasant enthusiasm is simply a matter of inexperience and ignorance. He is annoyed, but he must copulate with her if he is to have a legitimate heir. He fears an illegitimate son will be at greater risk from a pretender to his title. Of course, the Shogun would adjudicate contentious claims, but being no friend of the Shogun would certainly place his preferred heir in jeopardy.

"Ah shit, what is wrong with you anyway?" curses Mori in frustration.

"Wrong with me, my lord? Have I offended you?" responds Chizuru, surprised.

"Offended no. Provided me with a pleasant fuck, not at all! I can get more pleasure my from hand than from you!" blurts Mori angrily.

"I am sorry, my lord. I am unskilled at pillowing," responds Chizuru

"And unskilled you shall remain. Leave me now. Only return here on a day when you are fertile. Consult with the midwives. They will know. You must bear my heir."

At the shrine, in tearful prayer, Chizuru's *kami* reveals that she will bear no child, but that she will be the mother of many daughters. She is confused by this contradictory revelation. She, momentarily however, sets aside the contradiction because of her fear of Lord Mori when she reveals to him her barrenness.

"I don't know, my lord. Perhaps because of my fever. But I am certain that I can bear no child."

"No child! No child! Why have you deceived me? Why are you here? How long have you known, you bitch!"

"I was not certain, my lord. But it now seems that I am barren."

"Leave me! Do not return here. You are unwelcome in my presence and chambers," barks Lord Mori with finality.

Chapter Twenty-One
My Iron Rice Bowl

For three hundred years, peace imposed by the powerful Tokugawa Shogunate in *Yedo*, has prevailed in Japan. But after all these years, the hereditary regime is beginning to crumble. The isolationist *sakoku* policy is fraying at the edges; there is economic anxiety due to the country's coinage being steadily devalued, the *daimyo*, while overtly compliant to the edits from *Yedo*, are becoming more restive, and "Dutch learning," officially illegal, is popular, providing the closed country with not only limited trade with the West but opportunities in linguistics, cross-culturalism, and technology. Although the Jesuits, the Franciscans, and their Japanese followers were effectively and thoroughly exterminated in the mid-seventeenth century, pragmatically the *bakufu* allow the less evangelical, commerce-oriented Dutch to continue to operate out of *Dejima* Island, near *Nagasaki*. Their small, unobtrusive presence, along with the aforementioned and many other factors, has eroded *Yedo's* iron-grip on Japan. The regime's efforts at reform and modernization are resisted by feudal conservatives and scoffed at by liberal reformers alike. A revolution is in the making.

Just shy of two years has passed since Okada, Jiro and Takeshi boarded Commodore Perrys' flagship, the *USS Mississippi*, and departed for foreign lands. On their voyage they have traveled by steam-powered vessels, both blue water and riverine, rail and carriage. They have traversed their host country and seen ports in Mexico and the Republic of Colombia. They have listened, learned and imitated their Caucasian hosts. Okada is dead, a result of miscalculation, obstinacy and racism, but Jiro and Takeshi have returned to Japan with a wealth of experience and insight which the *bakufu* so desperately needs in order to treat with these foreign devils and which both Jiro and Takahashi will leverage into position and prestige within the *gaimusho*, foreign office, of the regime.

From the deck of the *USS Savannah*, Jiro and Takeshi stand gawking at snow-capped Mount Fuji and the panoramic landscape of Tokyo Bay as the ship glides through its calm waters toward the pier.

"Oh, by the gods it is good to see Japan! I will never again leave its shores," exclaims Takeshi.

"I agree, Takeshi, it's been a long voyage. I look forward to just routine normalcy again. Soon upon return, however, I must travel down the *Michinoku* Road to *Gonohe* to honor my family. I wonder if my parents and brothers are still alive?" ponders Jiro.

"I'm sure they are fine, Jiro. It hasn't been that long. We've only been away two years. I can't wait to eat *onigiri* again. Lots of soft, white rice, grilled squid, chicken skewers and pickles, just think of it! And no more stew. Never again stew!"

"You're indeed making me hungry, Takeshi. Stop it. It'll be a couple of hours yet before we are ashore, and I'm so hungry for Japanese food."

"We should go back to *Yoshiwara*, don't you think? With the gold *koban* we'll be paid, and being government men now, they'll have to be nice to us. I'm getting horny and hungry."

"Two constants in life, Takeshi. You being horny and hungry. The world is evenly balanced on the back of the turtle!" sophisizes Jiro.

The along the eastern edge of *Tokyo* Bay, piers and long warehouses line the shore. The *Savannah* is met some hundreds of yards from shore by an indigenous long boat carrying a harbor pilot. Once aboard, his instructions being interpreted by Jiro, he guides the vessel into port to a berth and official delegation. The other two escort vessels of Commodore Mervine's small flotilla are ordered to anchor in the harbor.

Jiro and Takeshi are among the first to disembark, along with several naval officers including the Commodore. They are ceremoniously greeted, and to everyone's surprise, the Americans are asked to remain aboard their vessel until an official meeting can be arranged within the next several days. The Commodore may provide a written list of requested resupply to the harbor master. The meeting is ended, and Jiro and Takeshi depart with the greeting party. Their two year foreign journey is at an end; they are returned to Tokugawa Japan.

The greeting delegation returns to the foreign office building, some several *ri* distant, by *jinrikusha*. Taking in the sights, smells and sounds of "home," the duo hardly think ahead to their debriefing, new careers and lives from this day forward.

Takeshi gushes. "Japan! *Yedo*! Home! Jiro, this is the happiest day of my life!"

"Happy, yes, but our lives will be different now. We are no longer part of our lord's stable. We are no long students of the *Yushima Seido*. We are part of the system now, functionaries in the *bakufu*. We should congratulate ourselves, but the unknowns are many and I'm not sure what even later today will bring. I only know for certain that you, Takeshi, are my friend and that the regime and our new positions in it will become our future. This will be my iron rice bowl."

"Wow, that's pretty heady, Jiro. I just want to eat."

"Yes, Taka-san, I agree. First I want a long, hot Japanese bath. I'll scrub myself raw and remove every wisp of foreign stink."

"Yes, I'll take a big shit and pass out every morsel of navy stew," interjects Takeshi.

"Right. After our big shits, our plan of action is: off with these clothes, into a hot bath, and fill our bellies with delicious Japanese food and sake until we puke."

"Let's do it!"

On the first day of the debrief, Jiro and Takeshi, an inseparable duo for the past two years, are separated. They are instructed not to meet, greet or speak with one another until the debrief process is finished. They have no choice but to comply.

In a bare room within the *gaimusho*, Jiro is seated before his "interrogators." There are three. Two men sit directly in front of Jiro, one stands back, observing the other two. Jiro is offered tea.

"Let us begin with life aboard their ships. Tell us all that you are able, Ueno Jiro," demands the first interrogator.

"The *gaijin* ships are large, larger than any Japanese vessel. They have masts for sail, but their primary source of propulsion is coal-fired steam engines. The engines are essentially huge iron pots filled with water, heated to produce steam, which drives pistons, which in-turn propel the vessel by paddles or screw," explains Jiro to his already confused interrogators.

"Can you sketch the system which you are describing, Ueno Jiro?"

"Yes, I think I can. But it will have to be from memory. I was not allowed to make drawings of their equipment and such while aboard."

"I see. Their armaments?"

"There are many types of *gaijin* ships. They are organized into classes of ships. Each ship in a given class is similar but not identical. They seem to be armed according to the size and class of ship. We were on two different types of naval vessel. First, the *USS Mississippi*, named for a great river in the center of their country. The *Mississippi* was a paddle-driven steam ship. This ship carried only ten guns. These guns were large. I could fit both of my fists, side by side, into the barrel of the gun, and they were larger still! These were newer Paixhans guns, the first naval gun capable of carrying explosive shells. We witnessed a demonstration of these guns. Incredibly dangerous! The second vessel, the *USS Powhatan*, also a paddle-driven vessel. This ship carries sixteen guns, eleven of which are the big Dalgren guns. They have an unusual shape, supposedly for safety. They fire solid, exploding and canister shot. Also very dangerous guns."

"You sound as those you admire these foreign devils?"

"No sir, I do not. But I do admire their technology, their country and its industrial might. They are not to be underestimated," replies Jiro defensively. "The American *gaijin* themselves are quite different than other foreigners with whom Japan has dealt. In China, Korea, Portugal and Holland, these people are all related in one manner or another. In America, they are as different as fish in the sea. Some are big, and hairy, others are small and quick. There are a few who pride themselves on fine clothes and cleanliness, others who are uncouth and filthy. As a people they generally worship the God of the Cross, but there are those who worship nothing but money and themselves. They build beautiful cities and monuments, and the vastness of their country is without end. All of these things paint an interestingly complex picture of the American *gaijin*. Unlike we Japanese however, they lack unity, harmony and dignity. The question is whether Japan in the midst of western-driven economic and industrial revolution can survive only on unity, harmony and dignity."

For several days the "interrogation of Jiro continues. When the *gaimuhso* functionaries had finished, Jiro is offered a lucrative job within the *bakufu*.

In 1856 Harris Townsend arrives as the first United States Counsel General in Japan. This first American Consulate is located at the Gyokuzen-ji temple in *Shimoda*. Some three years later, a reciprocal mission from Japan is sent to establish the first Japanese Consulate in San Francisco.

Ueno Jiro is assigned to work the "American" desk within the *gaimusho*. He is tasked to work with a young naval officer, Lieutenant Sugiyama, with whom he is partnered for the next number of years.

Some years later, now *Kaigun Shosa*, Lt. Commander Sugiyama instructs Harbor Pilot Noi and "Interpreter" Ueno Jiro standing before him on the wharf. "Bring these *keito*, white niggers, into port. Let us see what we can learn today."

Chapter Twenty-Two
Command

Secretary of the Navy
William A. Graham

To all who shall see these presents greeting: Know ye that reposing special trust and confidence in the patriotism, valor, fidelity and abilities in Lieutenant David S. McDougal, USN, he is hereby appointed to command of the sloop of war, *USS Warren*. The appointment shall continue at the pleasure of the President of the United States by whose the authority of this order is given. Said command shall become effective this 15th day of June 1852.

Lieutenant McDougal sits quietly in his cabin aboard the *USS Warren* and reads the command order once again. How sweetly it reads. At long last, twenty-six years after reporting aboard the *USS Congress* as a Midshipman, David finally commands his own ship. True, it is not a pirate chasing, gun-dueling first ship of the line of his dreams, rather an aging sloop of war with a history of mutiny. They say that there has never been a mutiny aboard a United States Ship, but this depends, of course, how you precisely define mutiny. For a moment, David ponders how he would react to mutinous sailors aboard his ship. The best way, of course, is to run a healthy, clean and tight ship, never allowing the crew to sink into melancholy, despair and ill-disciplined behavior. Leaving that thought for the moment, David picks up his quill and pens a letter to his bride of six weeks.

Dear Katherine,

How bitter-sweet this moment. After a lifetime of study, training and always playing second fiddle, I am now in sweet command of my own ship. MY ship, the USS Warren is an older ship, laid down in Boston in the late '20s. But she is a true sailing sloop, which are becoming harder and harder to find in this man's steam-powered navy. I will enjoy reacquainting myself with wind and sail. The vessel has a checkered history, but I intend to write my own.

The bitter in this moment is my unhappiness at leaving you. After only a few happy weeks together, we are parted for who knows how long. I, here in Norfolk, until I receive orders and you there in Leonardstown. We are but a few leagues apart, a day's sail perhaps, yet in two separate worlds.

I love you Katherine, I always have. I must do my duty, I always will. By the grace of Providence, I will return to your loving arms as soon as the Navy permits. Be strong my love.

Your loving husband, David

David does not have to wait long for his orders. He is ordered to rejoin the Pacific Squadron near San Francisco.

```
Secretary of the Navy
William A. Graham
```

```
To Lieutenant David S. McDougal,
Commander USS Warren. Proceed, at
earliest opportunity, from Port Nor-
folk, Virginia to Mare Island, State
of California. The USS Warren is
hereby detached from the U.S. Home
Squadron and upon arrival, reat-
tached to the U.S. Pacific Squadron
effective upon receipt of this mes-
sage. In transit you are designated
as an Independent Command. Standing
orders on anti-piracy, freedom of
navigation and protection of Ameri-
can lives and property apply. You
```

are to carry a full load of naval
stores intended for the U.S. Pacific
Squadron for disbursement and use at
the discretion of its Commanding Officer.

Good luck and Godspeed.

David seats himself. He is momentarily stunned. He reads the
order again, more slowly. When finished for the second time, he
sits there talking to himself. "Independent command! What a
lucky draw. Easy sailing through the Caribbean, down past Brazil
Station, these are familiar waters. Continue south, then south by
west, Buenos Aires and around the Horn of South America, Cape
Horn. This, a cold and miserable challenge. The contrary winds,
towering waves, icy and unforgiving cold and all the time, the
West Wind Drift fighting us all the way. But, once around the
Horn, we ride the Peru Current almost all the way to California.
Many have gone before me. I can do this."

David stops and thinks about his new bride, Katherine, in
Leonardstown. "Another letter? I think not. Not now. I'll write
it later. Post it from Brazil outbound. She'll understand. She'll
have to understand. She is a Navy wife now!"

Lieutenant McDougal has approximately two months to become acquainted with the capabilities of his ship and crew before
his run around The Horn. On average the Warren will do five
knots, covering a distance of seven thousand miles excluding re-
provisioning in ports, as necessary, along the way. McDougal reasons that this should be sufficient time for observation and any

corrections to routine or procedure. Battle preparedness and gunnery will not rank high on his list of priorities, in that the Warren is a stores ship and no longer considered a first-line combatant, even a secondary combatant for that matter. Nevertheless, a prudent measure of general preparedness will include firefighting, general quarters and test firing all of Warren's twenty, thirty-two pound guns.

Given his previous experience in the region, McDougal and the Warren set a direct course from Norfolk to Port of Spain, Trinidad, the Warren's first port of call. He'll take on water, fresh fruit, vegetables and post the ship's mail. His letter to Katherine will be part of that post.

Dear Katherine,

We are underway! The Warren has been ordered to rejoin the Pacific Squadron at Mare's Island in the new State of California. I am uncertain as to subsequent missions, but will write you at first opportunity.

The ship handles well. She and her crew are well seasoned, so I am not expecting many surprises. We make on average five knots per hour, more if the wind and currents are right. It is over fourteen thousand miles from Norfolk to San Francisco, but my only real concern is Cape Horn at the tip of South America. The winds are often contrary, and the seas rough, but I am confident in my navigation, the soundness of the ship and the abilities of my crew. All will be well.

I do not worry so much about you with your family at hand. Do not worry about me, I am skilled and God is good. Until we meet again, my love.

Your adoring husband, David

The *Warren*'s cruise to California goes as well as can be expected in a thirty year- old wooden vessel. The only tense moments occur on the Pacific side, off Punta Arenas, Chile at 53.14 degrees south, when the *Warren* springs a serious leak, due no doubt to the incessant pounding she took in making her run around the Horn. After some hard hours on the bilge pumps and an impermanent repair by the skilled hands of the Chief Carpenter, the Warren is sufficiently sea-worthy to continue her mission to California.

Bilge pumps and the ship's Chief Carpenter however cannot undo the marital damage of David's second letter to Katherine. After only a few months as Mrs. Katherine McDougal, a bride's remorse descends on Katherine.

"How could I have, Mother? How could I have agreed to marry that sea-loving bellhop. 'Be strong, Katherine.' Be strong to what end? He's gone now for how long? When will he return? And then gone again. I did not marry a husband, I married a pen-pal. Oh, Mother, what should I do? What can I do?" laments Katherine at the receipt of the letter from Port of Spain.

For his part, Lieutenant David McDougal, having dutifully penned a letter to his wife, clearly explaining his mission and duty, places domestic issues aside and focuses on his mission, ship and crew.

At the Naval Shipyard of Mare Island, some twenty-three miles northeast of San Francisco, California, Lieutenant McDougal brings the *USS Warren* into berth. His first command cruise is a success. Given the great distances and conveyance options available, furlough is not possible and the young Lieutenant is soon given orders to take command of the recently overhauled *USS Hancock*, one of the first of its kind in the U.S. Navy, a steam-powered tugboat. It is an intimate and hardly a fighting command with a tight crew of only twenty souls and one small deck gun. The Hancock is ordered west, to navigate unknown seas, chart large islands off Southeast Asia and to develop friendly relations Oriental nations. As always, American political reason dictates that good show the American flag would deter piracy thereby promoting commerce and protecting American lives and property. The *Hancock* is further ordered to rendezvous Commodore Perry's' Japan Squadron and render any assistance required thereby.

Ignoring a growing sense of concern about his domestic relations, confident in doing his duty for both hearth and country, David embarks on his new command and steams west to the port of Hong Kong via *Yedo* in Japan.

The four thousand five hundred nautical mile route to *Yedo* should take the Hancock a little more than twenty-seven days if not impeded by foul weather or repair. The tug is overloaded with coal and sustenance for its engine and crew as it steams west to rendezvous.

The *Hancock* joins with Commodore Perry's Japan Squadron laying at anchor off *Yedo*. After the signing of the Convention of Kanagawa, Lieutenant McDougal and the Hancock continue their mission west first to Busan, then on to Hong Kong. In

Hong Kong, Lieutenant McDougal leaves the *Hancock* and joins the officers of the *USS Mississippi*, thereby returning to the United States with the Commodore's squadron.

On furlough, David tries to mend his short, but already broken marriage. His prolonged naval missions, brief letters and the inherent differences between David and Katherine in the great national debate over States Rights, abolition and the status of the Negro, have all but destroyed a union brought together by only mild physical and personality attraction.

At long last, in 1862, in the midst of our national fratricidal bloodletting, now Commander David S. McDougal is awarded command of a modern and powerful fighting ship, the *USS Wyoming*. The *Wyoming*, like many warships of the era, is a hybrid of both steam and sail. She is a new design however, laid down in 1858 possessing a propulsion system of engine, shaft and propeller capable of eleven knots. She has only six guns, three of which are older thirty-two pounders, two large eleven-inch Dalgren guns, and one highly accurate sixty pound Parrott rifle. There is no need for more guns. Deadly explosive ordnance and accuracy have replaced old-fashioned naval broadsides.

```
Secretary of the Navy
Gideon Welles


To Commander David S. McDougal, Com-
mander USS Wyoming. You are to pro-
ceed to Japan via the Sandwich
Islands (also known as Hawaii),
```

there to expect further information
on cruising the waters off Southeast
Asia. Your primary mission is to
find, seize and/or sink the Confed-
erate-flagged commerce raider, *CSS
Alabama*. You will of course inter-
dict piracy and provide assistance
to American merchantmen, particularly the whaling fleet in south-
central Pacific.

Godspeed and good hunting!

David is elated. "Another independent command! True, a potentially long and indefinite mission in far-away waters, but a real
mission, not just wallowing off Southern ports trying to catch a
blockade runner or two. There is not much glory to be found as
one of dozens of ships of General in Chief Winfield Scott's so-
called Anaconda Plan fleet blockading, 'strangling' the South in
submission and another source of friction with Katherine. Yes,
Katherine. What to do about Katherine? Well, there is nothing
to be done. Duty calls, and I will answer its call."

Commander David S. McDougal, the *USS Wyoming* and her
crew of 198 souls depart Mare Island, California and steam west
toward Japan and their destiny.

Some weeks later, in his cabin aboard the Wyoming, now entering Japanese waters, David writes a heart-felt letter to his es-
tranged wife, Katherine.

Dear Katherine,

Let us not quarrel. How is it that only a few short years ago, we were lovingly staring into each other's eyes professing with our lips the profound love of our hearts. And now, we find ourselves at odds over political rhetoric. My heart longs for the adoring, giggling Katherine of my youth. My lips still desire to taste the sweetness of thy kiss. I still love you my dear!

Even as I serve in the uniform of the republic of my birth, I know there exists some youthful, straw-haired and debonair cavalier plying, not unrewarded, for they attentions. Is it our quarrelling, is it the fantasies of so young an admirer or the allure of his allegiance to the idyllic plantations of thy youth? For the love of Christ Katherine, your father has had no slaves since before our courtship. Why is it then that the legal status of these nappy-headed niggers should matter so much and come between us? I am not an abolitionist, neither am I a traitor to my country. Make me understand my dear. My heart breaks for thee. I am at a loss for understanding?

When this war has consumed all around it so that it is self-extinguished, I will return to you and my Maryland. If there is a token tied, hanging from the porch, I will enter and fall down on my knees begging you forgiveness for being away so long a time and pleading for your love again. In the absence of such a token, I will ride on and return to the sea, if she will have me.

Until that day my dearest Katherine, may the Lord our God keep thee from all sickness and harm and I will hold thee in my heart.

Your most devoted husband,
David

Chapter Twenty-Three
Seek Revenge and Dig Two Graves

*E*vents have changed the character of young Lord Mori Takachika. The pressures, real or imagined, of being the thirteenth in a prodigious line of powerful *daimyo* are great. So too is the trauma of having survived what he believes to have been an assassination attempt on his life by his father's enemies. The untimely death of his father from a maybe-not-so-accidental spider bite as well as bearing witness to the beginnings of the collapse of the centuries-old feudal system and the ruling regime, all have worked to twist what may have been a normal young lordling into an angry, paranoid, and sometimes violent ruling lord.

It is clear to Takachika what he has and doesn't have in this life. He has inherited a large and influential domain, and the leadership of an old and respected *han*. The symbol of his power is the "widow-maker" sword which never leaves his sight. He reveres his Emperor, the *Mikado*, who remains cloistered away in

Kyoto and longs for his direct rule, with, of course, the advice and consent of the supporting *daimyo*. What he does not have are friends and allies whom he can trust and a wife who will bear him an heir. He is the end of his line, unless he begets bastards by proxy, which, of course, he will, but whose claim to the domain weakens with every generation.

"Takahashi, take note. We must organize and regiment the domain for maximum economic and political strength. All commercial and private activities are to be approved and supervised to the benefit of this house. We shall not call it taxation; the word makes men angry and restive. We shall simply put the house forward as rightful owner to all such activities within the boundaries of the domain. This is my birthright!"

"Yes, my lord, but this has never been done before. There may be complications," cautions Counselor Takahashi.

"Of course, that is why you will coordinate this with the *daijin* and incorporate them into the scheme. As active participants they will have no choice but to support these activities."

"Very clever, my lord."

"Further, you will seek out and cultivate direct contacts with the Imperial court in *Kyoto*. It is important that any of our more controversial activities be cloaked with the legitimacy of the Imperial court. The dogs in *Yedo* may not be pleased with our, more independent course. Lastly, send for my uncle, Akane and Tamura. When they are assembled, we shall discuss our military options."

"Yes, my lord. These things shall be done." Counselor Takahashi, with a deep bow, exits the Takahashi's chamber.

At a later date, Lord Mori meets in private chamber with an assembly of his uncle, Mori Masamitsu; Akane Takito; Tamura Saburo; and Counselor Takahashi.

"Gentleman, we are gathered here to discuss the military organization of the domain. As you are aware, *Hagi* Castle is one of the greatest fortifications in western Japan. This is the base of our *han* and the center of the domain. Much work has already been accomplished in the collectivization of economic activities in the domain. This has already greatly increased our treasury which, in turn, provides us with more options.

"The peasants are our greatest asset. Every young man of the domain will be required to attend martial instruction for a period of one season. This will not adversely affect crop production, but will provide the domain with a reserve of men should these be required in the future. Secondly, each of you will choose the best of these trainees to be members in a standing force of infantry, cavalry and seaborne forces. Uncle, as overall commander, you will choose artillery specialists from amongst your infantry regiment."

Takachika continues:

"Akane, your great family, love of horses and superb horsemanship make you the natural choice to lead my cavalry. Cavalry shall not be used only as a means of conveyance by the *daijin*, but as a reconnaissance and shock force. We shall require several hundred good mounts. Use the merchants, teach them a bit about equine and start buying up all the horses you can in the surrounding domain. Finally, you Tamura. Your knowledge of smuggling and piracy will make us masters of both the Inland Sea and the Sea of Japan. The three vessels we received from *Yedo*, the "goodwill" token from their barbarian friends, these will be the core of our forces afloat. Observe the foreign vessels transiting the Inland Sea and the *Shimonoseki Strait*. Mimic their maneuvers, learn from them. The barbarian *gaijin* have much more experience at sea than we."

Counselor Takahashi brings forth the questions the others think.

"My lord, what is the ultimate purpose of assembling such a powerful force? *Yedo* is too weak, opinions too divided and too far away for much interference from them. Invasion? Do you intend to invade a neighboring domain?"

"Takahashi, Takahashi, always the worrier. Yes, *Yedo* is too weak and too far away. I do not expect much interference from them. And no, I do not intend to invade a neighboring domain, although I would like to rid the world of the groveling dogs in *Okayama*. We will position our forces forward along the coast of the Inland Sea and the *Shimonoseki Strait*. We will deny free passage and exact a heavy toll from any transiting vessel. Our fortifications and forces will deter our enemies and make the transit toll a reasonably cheap alternative to hostile action against us. Only our reserve force and home guard will reside in the environs of *Hagi* Castle."

Counselor Takahashi, the worrier, has, as directed, cultivated contacts with the Imperial Court in *Kyoto*, but seeing the reckless direction of the young Lord of the *Choshu*, has also opened covert communications with the *bakufu* via *Shikimi*.

Over the next decade, Takachika dramatically reforms the economy and administration of the *Choshu* Domain, but these gains are somewhat offset by his obsession with military preparedness and minor incursions and interference in the affairs of his neigh-bors. Traditionally and always an enemy of the *bakufu*, his activ-ities are monitored carefully in *Yedo*.

After the Convention of Kanagawa in 1854, some restive *daimyo*, particularly the *Choshu* and *Satsuma* Domain, use the concessions given to foreign powers as a rallying cry in their on-going struggle with the regime in *Yedo*. These *daimyo* are quick to point out that the Imperial Court is not in favor of the Convention and that the regime in *Yedo* signed and agreed to its terms only under duress, that is, under the guns of Com-modore Perry's flotilla. This then becomes a movement of some strength, the *Sonno Joi*, Revere the Emperor, Expel the Barbarians, movement which culminates in an official Imperial Decree to that end in 1864.

By 1863 a confluence of events; a decade of military prepara-tions, a further weakening of the regime in *Yedo* and under the guise of the *Sonno Joi* movement, Lord Mori Takachika strikes by effectively closing the *Shimonoseki Straits* to non-Japanese vessels, both commercial and naval.

Mori Takachika, the current ruler and thirteenth *daimyo* of the clan, sits ceremoniously erect on a colorful *zabuton* in the great hall of *Hagi* Castle. Two perpendicular lines of *daijin* of the realm similarly seated, are intently listening. Mori *tono* speaks quietly but with the force of a brewing storm.

"*Tennoheika ga*, His Imperial Majesty, has decreed *Joi jikko no chokumei*, order to expel the barbarians, that all these pestilent foreigners should be expelled from the sacred homeland by no later than the tenth day of the fifth month. We, the Mori clan, will not feign from our sacred duty to his Imperial Majesty. *Sonno Joi!* Make all necessary preparations. Preparations for holy war against the barbarian."

Chapter Twenty-Four
State and the Struggle

"Thomas Jefferson was a republican. A republican in the sense that he embraced the notion of a democratic republic of the people. Being wealthy and a slave owner were more a legacy of his family and his times rather than a reflection on his political and moral philosophy," explains Seward.

"How do you then view this new party, Bill? asks Robert.

"I see the new Republican Party as an amalgamation of anti-slavery, modernizers, ex-Whigs and ex-Free Soilers. Ohio Senator Salmon P. Chase sums up the new Republican Party as 'free labor, free land and free men.' I can think of no better words," reflects Seward.

"Does the Party stand a chance in New York? Nationally?" queries Robert.

"Founded in Wisconsin in 1854, it held its first Convention in Michigan only a few months later. Now, it already dominates most of the northern states. The Whigs are dead. In spite of notable leadership, the Whigs have not changed with the times. Their big loss in opposing the Kansas-Nebraska Act proves them to be an ineffective voice against the Democrats. The Abolitionists and Free Staters won't work with them any longer. The Republicans unite all these factions and more under one banner," expounds Seward.

"These are troubling times, Bill. Who knows where it will all end? Stephan Douglas is a Democratic hero, but still the Deep South doesn't trust him, no doubt just because he hails from Illinois. The Know-Nothings are raising hell, particularly here in New York, and the Western Expansionists just don't care. 'Free Land' is their mantra. The nation seems to be tearing apart. It is sectionalism at its worst!" laments Robert.

"I couldn't agree with you more, Bill. That's why we need to unify these factions, these sections under one Party. If we don't, the Republic is doomed," states Seward firmly.

"A sore subject I am certain, but I think our friendship is strong enough for a direct and honest exchange of views. Do you really think that a close relationship with Thurlow Weed is good for you politically, in the long term?"

"Weed? Well, that's a good question. Thurlow has been around forever. He was the kingmaker of the Whigs. But, in retrospect, the Whigs' record itself isn't so impressive. In New York though, shunning Thurlow would be political suicide. On the national level, being seen close to him may result in the same sudden death. A conundrum for certain. In any event, it is too late now. He supported me in 54' and is already in the Republican mix. We'll see what kind of pudding we bake."

Although no longer with the New York State Assembly, Robert makes the political migration with his friend William Seward over to the Republican Party. He follows his friend's political ascension with interest.

As avid abolitionists both William and Robert are horrified yet pleased with John Brown's raid on the United States Arsenal at Harper's Ferry. Some of their friends have covertly provided both moral and material support to the insurgency. True, John Brown's slave rebellion has failed; yet in his failure, its tempest has demonstrated the urgency of a national reconciliation on the issue of this "peculiar institution." John Brown's "work" in the Kansas Territory—his raid, trial and execution—has contributed to the national debate, but more importantly to the presidential elections of 1860.

No one but everyone is prepared for the Great Republican Convention of 1860. The field is crowded with a host of candidates vying to carry the Republican banner into the election. Chicago is chosen as the venue, but Chicago, a city of only one hundred-ten thousand souls, has no facility large enough for the expected ten thousand delegates and attendees.

Seward and Pruyn make their plans to travel together to the Convention as Chicago rushes to build the Wigwam, a two story, temporary wooden structure built in just over one month to host the convention.

"Bill, are you familiar with the proposed Party platform?"

"I've managed to see a draft copy. Judge William Jessup and I go back a lot of years. I wonder though how many of the others, 'go back a lot of years with the judge'?" ponders Seward.

"Senator Salmon Chase for sure!" interjects Robert.

"Yes, the good Senator Chase, I am sure. In any case, the Platform is straightforward and unabashed. It is clearly abolitionist, that is, free soil, anti-slavery, opposing the Fugitive Slave Act, and, of course, the preservation of the Union," continues Seward.

"The preservation of the Union. How many Southern delegates do you expect?" asks Robert.

"All are welcome, but I'd be surprised if anyone from the Deep South attended, maybe a few from Border States such a Virginia, Kentucky and Missouri," states Seward.

"Can we prevail in a national election without support from any of the Southern States?"

"Yes, today it is possible. It would not have been possible in elections past, but right now the country is deeply divided. There will be no single Democratic candidate. Breckinridge will probably carry the banner for the Deep South. Illinois' Douglas should become the official Democratic endorsee. Of course, the Know-Nothings will rally a few malcontents and the Republicans will stand by the Union. Who knows about any others. That is why we will win!"

"A brilliant summation Bill. It is no wonder that you are the leading Republican candidate. President William H. Seward, sounds good, eh?"

"The nomination is a few weeks, but a lifetime away. Let's get packed and start working our way across the great heartland of the country to Chicago!"

Boarding a New York Central westbound, the pair take over a month to travel from Albany to Chicago. Embarking and disembarking their First Class coach all along the mainline, boarding short lines or riding carriages, they visit smaller towns and townships spreading the good news of the Republican Party rising up to save the Union. William, being the leading candidate and expected to win the Republican nomination, receives a heartening welcome at most every stop. But, as the leading candidate of the staunchly abolitionist Republicans, he is, unbeknownst to him, being followed and marked for death.

The Fire-Eaters are a group of extremist pro-slavery Southern Democrats led by Robert Rhett of South Carolina. They have decided to send a strong message to the new Republican Party and its supporters that they are a force to be reckoned with.

"Louis, the council has decided to silence William Seward. He is presently traveling from Albany to Chicago with only a friend and a secretary. Send a trusted man. Make sure the assassination is bloody and public. I'll make sure the Mercury runs an editorial sympathetic to our cause and a fitting obituary to Senator Seward. The talk of their Convention will be less about abolition and more about who is next," instructs Robert Rhett.

"I'll send Karl. His German ancestry and accent will blend in well in Ohio. He is good with a gun, knife or hands, it doesn't matter. Karl's our man," responds Louis without even considering the moral aspects of murder.

"Port Clinton, Ohio. We'll purge the country of one more sanctimonious windbag in Port Clinton, Ohio. Chase's territory. We rid ourselves of Seward and severely embarrass Chase. What could be better?"

On a beautiful late spring day, Seward and Pruyn board a local train for the short hop from Sandusky, Ohio, to Port Clinton along Lake Erie. The twenty-mile journey will take less than one hour.

Seward is expected and a friendly crowd meets his coach trackside. As he steps down from the train, a burly, mean-looking man approaches from an otherwise typical and unremarkable group. Instinctively Seward steps back as the report of the pistol startles all. The six-inch backstep is just enough for the bullet to miss his torso and bore a hole in his sleeve. Seward is unharmed, while Robert, the military man, pulls a derringer from within his overcoat and leaps after the would be assassin. Karl melts back into the crowd of townspeople and disappears into a saloon.

Some minutes later an out-of-breath Robert rejoins William Seward on the station platform.

"Well, that was lucky for being unlucky. The whole idea of becoming the President just became a little less attractive to me," states William flatly and without emotion.

"I wonder who and why?" questions Robert.

"Some little man from the South I would imagine, Robert. The bigger question, of course, is who sent him. We already know the why. Our strong and unwavering positions on not returning fugitive slaves, that is **property**, to their 'rightful' owners and abolition have always made us enemies, but as a candidate for President, or as President, the message to the nation is much louder. The Struggle is already begun. The South will fight," predicts William.

At the Republican Convention in the Wigwam, William leads the other nine candidates for the nomination on the first two ballots. The assassination attempt in Port Clinton has, however, temporarily doused some of the fire in his belly. This slight lack of enthusiasm does not go unnoticed. A perceptive David Davis, the campaign manager for Abraham Lincoln, redoubles his effort in promoting his "quiet man" candidate as a less incendiary choice and a Unionist who can hold the country together. The Convention sees this wisdom in this, at least for the time to take one ballot, thereby making "dark horse" Abraham Lincoln its nominee for President in 1860.

Lincoln wins the 1860 election amidst a high voter turnout but with only forty percent of the vote. He carries not one Southern or Border state. A cumulative dissatisfaction with the Union, the elections and the Republican platform more than the man Lincoln drive the South to secession. As predicted by William Seward months before, The Struggle has begun and will not end until millions have bled and Lincoln is dead.

President Lincoln is a wise man. He believes in the proverb attributed to Machiavelli, "keep your friends close and your enemies closer." In doing so, Seward, among others, becomes a member of the Lincoln Cabinet. He is chosen by the President to be his Secretary of State.

Robert, as a general officer in the New York State Militia, begins to prepare his men for the war he knows is coming. But Robert will never taste the acrid smoke and bitter blood of The Struggle, rather he is promoted by Seward and selected by the President to represent the United States as its Representative Minister to the Court of the Shogun in Japan.

Just as the first skirmishes of The Struggle take place in Virginia and Missouri, Robert embarks on a mail packet steamer to Panama, crosses the Isthmus by rail, and continues by steamer to San Francisco. In San Francisco he pays a courtesy call on the new Japanese Consulate, and later boards a naval vessel bound for Japan, where he will spend the next four years of his life. He is unaware that he is following a route taken just a few years before by the first Japanese guests of the United States. His diplomatic path will soon cross and become intertwined with that of former guest, "Interpreter" Ueno Jiro of the Japanese *gaimusho*.

Two years later, Robert will meet the intrepid Commander David S. McDougal at the diplomatic Mission in Japan.

"Commander McDougal? I've been anxious to meet you. My name is Pruyn, Robert Hewson Pruyn. I am the Representative Minister to the Court of the Shogun and ultimately the *Mikado*, here in Japan. I, that is we, represent American interests here. I do apologize for the unseemly appearance of our temporary home here. We were burned out, you know. No, I guess you wouldn't know. No doubt you were at sea when all of this happened."

Chapter Twenty-Five
An Abundant Life

*T*he cock crows. The shadowy light of the moon and stars still reign in the small hours of the morning. Chizuru and her maidens sleep soundly in comfortable *futon* laid upon *tatami*, two inch woven rice straw mats, set into the Cyprus-board floor on the third level of *Hagi* Castle. She lies dreamless, half-awake, half-asleep, stretching, curling, feeling the warmth of her own body captured between the covers.

Chizuru perceives a motion, she believes it to be a dream. Then she senses the motion again. A feeling of panic electrically jolts her body as she fears Lord Mori entering the room, crawling upon her and violating her however he wishes with his veined, throbbing **thing**. Any word, any resistance will result in a swift and painful rebuke. She is completely awake now, but Lord Mori is not upon her, beside her or even in the room. Was it a dream? Suddenly, a maiden screams. The floor undulates like a wave. The walls sway back and forth. Crashing noises, cries and screams are heard all around the castle grounds. *Jishin*, earthquake, rocks *Hagi* Castle.

Lasting only a minute or two, the damage visible in the morning light is massive. Many masonry walls and structures have given way, their roofs collapsed onto victims sleeping beneath. The wood and straw structures of the peasants fair better, in that these flexed with the earth and did not resist. Many hearths were cold, so fires are few, but smoke is in the air.

Without precedent or the consent of her lord, Chizuru organizes her maidens in order to provide assistance to those so in need.

Lord Mori looks down from his chamber window to the grounds encompassed within the castle walls. He observes the ministrations of Chizuru and her maidens, but does not intervene.

"Stupid bitch. She demonstrates her lack of noble blood for all to see. She has no business playing nurse-maid to the common people. They are of little consequence to the *han*. Their fate is with the gods," mumbles Lord Mori exasperated.

Throughout the day and the days that follow, even during frightening aftershocks, Chizuru assists those in need. First, she and her maidens attend those within *Hagi* castle, then later in its environs. Tirelessly they work until they themselves are almost as ragged and dirty as those they serve. In whispered voices, the peasants and others higher in the feudal order, look upon her as a *kamisama*, minor god, incarnate.

"Lady Mori has done wonderful things, my lord," states Counselor Takahashi.

"Lady Mori? You mean that slut that bears me no heir, and grovels amongst the peasant stock from which she sprang," growls Lord Mori.

"As you say, my lord. True, she is not noble. But she comes from a respected and well-connected family. She has done much credit to the house of Mori and is thought highly of by your people," counters Counselor Takahashi, much to the surprise of Lord Mori.

"Yes, her family is well connected, but well connected to whom? To the dogs in *Yedo*, I suspect. She was presented to my gullible father like a shrimp offered to a bream. He, in turn, forced her upon me. But I am not so naïve, as not to see her currying favor with the peasants, and others, *Takahashi*, and to suspect her loyalties lie not with me, but with *Shikimi*, the Ryozuji and even *Yedo*. But this conversation is not about Lady Mori, rather the status of repair to *Hagi* castle. How bad are the damages?" questions Lord Mori pointedly.

"The castle and the harbor are sound, my lord. Some foundation stones may have moved, but they are designed to glide upon one another. Some superficial damage here and there but nothing of consequence. Repairs are being made at this time," reports Counselor Takahashi.

"Good, keep me informed. You may go," closes Lord Mori.

Lord Mori sits quietly and ponders his future, and with him the future of the *han* and the domain.

After three days and nights Chizuru and her maidens rest. They sup, they bathe and by candlelight they talk. Chizuru confesses another voice.

"My *kami* has spoken to me. It clearly told me, '*you honor me when you demonstrate the love I have for all that I have created. I am with thee and have blessed thee with an abundant life.*'"

They smile, nod their heads in affirmation, weep and fall asleep in one another's arms.

Years pass. Chizuru has learned to trust in Counselor Takahashi. She finds in him a quiet fortitude and wisdom upon which she can depend. Occasionally, he also conducts "important messages beyond the confines of *Hagi* Castle," just as her father had advised. She has learned to avoid Lord Mori. Her barrenness has made it easier to avoid him, as he soon bored of her unenthusiastic pillowing. Every day she listens for a voice, she looks for a sign. She cannot forget the words, "*I have blessed you with an abundant life.*" Again, she remembers the words of her father, "*you must endeavor to persevere.*" So she waits

From a window high above the practice yard, Lady Mori observes the events below. Her presence is hidden by fluttering curtains. Rice powered face, painted lips, straight black hair, wrapped in hand-sewn silk, she moves slowly, in practiced *Noh*, traditional Japanese theatre, like movements. Though cloistered, she moves freely within *Hagi* castle. Her favorite spots are those away from public view, like the empty room above the great hall or the warm space behind the kitchen hearth. She sees much and hears more. She grieves for poor Captain Tamura, maybe not so much for the man, as for herself trapped in this barbaric *bushido* culture, a culture whereby the liege lord can condemn or execute as much for sport as for justice. Inwardly she mocks a culture in which saving face becomes more important than living a life. Here she is trapped in her role of womanly silence, surrounded by barbaric cruelty. A tear forms in her eye, but it too is trapped before it can run her makeup. She runs a brush across her *suzuli*, stone ink board, and returns to her poetry.

Epilogue

This is a fictional story of the lives of five individuals of disparate race, culture and social standing racing together toward a common destiny.

The story is placed into an accurately detailed historical setting, that is, late Tokugawan Japan and early mid-19th century America. All of the places, many of the events and peripheral characters are historical. Some of the historical chronologies have been either compressed or expanded to suit the story.

I have tried to present the racism, prejudices, chauvinism, and sexuality of the era, as well as exposing their contemporary vestiges. Conversely, hope, aspirations and a universal, living Creator who links us all should be equally evident.

I hope that the liberal usage of foreign words in the story enriches the reading experience rather than confuses and distracts.

From Across The Waters is a prequel story to *The Search*,
Available from Dorrance Publishing.

Look for the sequel story of Admiral David S. McDougal,
Representative Minister Pruyn, Lord Mori Takachika,
Master Spy Ueno Jiro, and Lady (Sister Agnes) Mori
and others in

Legacies Are Forever

Coming soon!

List of Characters

Ueno Jiro – Master spy of the Tokugawan regime. (Fictitious)

David S. McDougal – U.S. Naval Officer (Historical)

Mori Takachika – Thirteenth *daimyo* of the Mori clan (Historical)

Robert H. Pruyn – Lawyer, Judge, General and Diplomat (Historical)

Chizuru – Lady Mori. Patterned after historical Sister Agnes, a 17th century Japanese Catholic saint (Fictitious)

Okada, Jiro and Takeshi – Patterned after historical Ambassador Shinmi Masaoki, Vice Ambassador Muragaki Norimasa and Observer Oguri Tadamasa (Fictitious)

Katherine (Kowalski) McDougal – David McDougal's wife (Fictitious)

Counselor Takahashi – Advisor to the Mori clan (Fictitious)

Others – Senators William Seward and Salmon Chase, Rector Sokan, Commodores Perry and Mervine, Thomas Byard, Sec. of State William Marcy, Captain Thomas Leathers of the *Natchez V*, Captains Cooper and Duncan of the *USS John Adams* and *Lexington* respectively, Judge William Jessup, Political Boss Thurlow Weed, Fire-Eater Robert Rhett, Lincoln Campaign Manager David Davis *and* the girls of Yoshiwara and Green Street, Busan, Korea (Historical)

Glossary of Foreign Words Used

Dutch

Onze vader die in die hemel zijt – First two lines of the Lord's
Prayer
Uw naam worde geheiligd

French

Raison d'etre – Reason for being
Tour de force – Impressive performance, or great achievement
Voila – There you go

Japanese

Ah, so desu ka – Ah, I see
Arigato – Thank you
Asagohan – Lit. morning rice, breakfast.
Aiu – Japanese sweetfish
Bakamon – Idoit
Bakaero – Son of a bitch (profane)

Bakufu – Tokugawa-era government

Biboujintsukuri – Widow-maker

Bushi – Samurai warrior

Bushido – Samurai code

Chashitsu – Teahouse

Chinchin – coll. Penis

Daigaku no kami – Head of the chief educational institute of the state

Daijin – Headman

Daijobu desu. Shimpai shinai de kudasai – It's okay, don't worry.

Dojo – Practice ring

Fundoshi - Loincloth

Furoshiki – Cloth wrapper

Gaijin – Foreigner

Gaimusho – Foreign office

Geisha-san – Female entertainer

Genkan – Threshold of a home

Go – Chinese board game

Han – Clan

Hai – Yes

Hajimemashita – How do you do

Hakama – Traditional trousers

Hokku/Haiku – Japanese poetry

Isshuban – Small, silver Tokugawa-era coin

Ikubei – Coll. Let's go

Ishidouro – Stone lantern

Iwana – Brook Trout

Jinja – Shinto shrine

Jinrikusha – Taxi cart for one or two persons, pulled by hand

Joi jikko no chokumei – Order to "Revere the Emperor, Expel the Barbarians"

Jishin - Earthquake

Kabuki – Japanese theatre

Kaerimichi – The way back (home)

Kaiyabukiyane – Thatched-roof dwelling

Kakebuton – Bed cover

Kami – Spirit or god

Kamidana – Family shrine

Kamisama – Minor god

Kamishimo - Vest

Kashikomarimashita otosama – Yes, I completely understand honorable father.

Katana – Japanese long sword

Keito – White nigger

Kendo – Japanese Martial Art

Kisu – Small surf fish

Koban – Standard gold Tokugawa-era coin

Kode – Lit. Wrist. Kendo movement

Koku – A measure of rice to feed one man, one year

Kokugo – Japanese language

Konnichi wa, Noriko de gozaimasu – Good morning. I'm Noriko.

Koto – Japanese musical instrument

Kuen/Korakuen – Famous garden along the Aashi River in central Japan

Kuso - Shit

Maiko-san – Young female entertainer

Michinoku – Lit. End of the road. District in northern Japan

Mikan – Mandarin oranges

Misoshiru – Bean paste broth

Mitsuba-aoi mon – Hollyhock crest of the Tokugawa

Mon – Gate (sometimes Customs)

Mon – Crest

Mon – Small, bronze Tokugawa-era coin

Nihon Shoki – Chronicles of Japan 720 A.D.

Noh – Ancient Japanese theatre

Oban – Ghost festival (Memorial Day)

Obi – Cloth belt

Oda – Old west-central domain in Japan

Okaerinasai – Welcome back

Onigiri – Rice ball

Ooshi - Delicious

Ri – Chinese unit of measure. ½ kilometer.

Roju – Senior Tokugawa-era official

Sake – Rice wine

Sakoku – Japan isolation policy mid-17th – mid-19th centuries

Seiza – Traditional formal manner of sitting

Sembei – Rice cracker

Sensei – Teacher or master

Shaden – Shinto alter

Shikaiishi - Revenge

Shinai – Bamboo practice sword

Shofu - Whore

Shogun – Military dictator

Shoheizaka Gakumonjo – A 19th Century Neo-Confucian High School

Suzuri – Ink stone

Tadaima – Coll. just now. I'm home.

Takoyaki – Grilled octopus balls

Taifu - Typhoon

Tamagozake – Egg and sake home remedy

Tatami – Woven rice straw mat

Tono-sama – My lord

Tanto – Japanese short sword

Tennoheika ga – His Imperial Majesty

Tofu – Soybean paste (cakes)

Tohoku – Northern district of Japan

Tokaido – Great east-west road in Japan

Tokugawa – Rulers of Japan, 17th–19th centuries

Tomokaku – No questions, just come

Tsuki – Lit. Throat. Kendo movement

Tsukemono – Pickled vegetables

Unda – Coll. yeh

Wakarimashita – I understand

Yakiika – Grilled squid

Yakisakana – Grilled fish

Yedo – Modern Tokyo

Yedo jidai – Edo era

Yohei ninja – Mercenary ninja

Yoshiwara – Red light district south of Tokyo

Yukata – Light robe

Yushima Seido – Tokugawa-era academy for young government bureaucrats

Zabuton – Traditional Japanese cushion

Korean

Hwongyong hamnida – Welcome

Hanguma haminda ga - Do you speak Korean

Latin

Pro bono – For the good

Pro tempore - Temporary

Portuguese

Lingua portuguesa - Portuguese

Obrigado – Thank you

Sim - Yes